THE ELECTRIC COMEDY

THE ELECTRIC COMEDY

rolando perez

> ...on another note,
> here is another book,
> serious, literary, and
> scholarly
> for Eyu Rob,
> literally,
> Rolando
> 11/5/00
> one day before
> the Elections

cool grove press

Copyright ©2000 by Rolando Perez

All rights reserved under the International and Pan-American Copyright Conventions. Published in the United States by Cool Grove Press, an imprint of Cool Grove Publishing, Inc., New York.
328 Flatbush Avenue, Suite 302, Brooklyn, NY 11238
http://WWW.COOLGROVE.COM

Publishers Cataloging-in-Publication

Perez, Rolando.
　The electric comedy / by Rolando Perez.—1st ed.
　p. cm.
　Based on Dante's Divine comedy.
　LCCN : 00-130475
　ISBN : 1-887276-23-8
　1. Consumption (Economics)—Fiction. 2. Virtual reality—Fiction. 3. Automation—Social aspects—4. Civilization, Modern—Fiction. I. Dante Alighieri, 1265-1321. Divina commedia. II. Title.

PS3566.E69134E44 20000　　　　　　813.6
　　　　　　　　　　　　　　　　　QBI00-254

Acknowledgments
*Thanks to all my friends who gave of their time
to help with comments, suggestions, and proofreading
the early drafts of this book. As always, I am indebted to
them for their help and encouragement, but most of all,
for their friendship.*

My thanks to the family of Michele Perillo for
granting me permission to use his wonderful
artwork.

Front cover design by Rolando Perez
Book design by P.T. Hazarika and Rolando Perez

First Edition
Printed in the United States

Dedication

*For my friends and family,
per i miei amici in Cortona,
and for Rosa
con amor(e).*

Preface

If it is in fact true that ignorance is bliss, then it was certainly my own ignorance about the complexity of Dante's *Divine Comedy*, which made me think that it was at all possible to write a book such as the one you are about to read. For no one in his right mind would attempt to undertake such a task: fraught with so many risks and potential for outright failure.

The idea for *The Electric Comedy* came to me from an early reading of Dante's *Inferno* some thirteen years ago. For what first struck me about this great work, and then some time later about the rest of the *Commedia*, was all the politics contained within it. Since I had never read anything about the *Inferno*, and initially approached it not as a scholar but as a curious reader, I was surprised to find that it was totally different than anything I had imagined. Perhaps it's because I had expected a Catholic school version of the *Inferno*: peopled with masturbators, fornicators, and thieves. The kinds of people, the nuns told us, would end up engulfed in the fires of hell. Yet here was a work—as political as Plato's *Republic* or Machiavelli's *The Prince*—imbued with philosophy, religion, poetry, and mythology: critical of the politics of its time. And so mustering up some courage, I climbed upon the strong shoulders of Dante, to borrow the tripartite structure of his *Divine Comedy* and the form of the Canto, to write a work in which I would explore my own society. My little boat, however, would be quite different than Dante's. Drunk and without direction, it would take me, where it has taken everyone else in the twentieth century: everywhere and nowhere, only to begin its journey all over again at the 'end'.

But before I set foot on my drunken boat, I wanted to know this much: What was the most basic element that defined the twentieth century? What was it that gave it its political, social, religious, and economic dimension? The Greek philosopher Thales, the first Western metaphysician, said "the world is made of water." For that is what he considered the most basic and necessary element of life. So what would Thales have said about our century? After some consideration, it occurred to me, that the one thing that this century has depended on more than anything else—the most basic element that guarantees our social, political, religious, and economic lives, is nothing other than electricity: the divine entity of the last one hundred years, and the basic element of the *Inferno* in this *Comedy*.

The Italian futurist, Marinetti, who welcomed the world of electricity with open arms at the turn of the century, could almost be said to be the father of modernity or postmodernity: ready to turn his back on the past, ready to put an end to religion, to put an end to mythology, and to embrace the very nihilism that Nietzsche, the philosopher of our age, warned against. These worshippers of technology set themselves on the banks of the electric Lethe, offering to baptize the twentieth and twenty-first century with the electricity of forgetfulness: making our past and our origins irrelevant, as though this were possible or desirable.

I know that there are readers who will be put off by the amount of mythology in this book. And I know who they are. They are the inheritors of Marinetti, born in front of a computer screen. They believe in virtual reality, they believe that an image is the same thing as a human being—or worse yet, more important. They are the twenty year olds—the flies in the marketplace that Nietzsche writes about in *Zarathustra*—

who trade billions of dollars a day on Wall Street. They are the twenty year olds who start up multi-million dollar companies on the Internet overnight; and they are the readers, not of *The Electric Comedy*, but of *WIRED* magazine. This book is not for them. This a book for those who worship words, for word fetishists—those who believe in the divinity of the word.

One of the great misconceptions of modernity, and especially of American culture, is the belief that one can have a society of any depth or significance without memory, without history, without myths, without poetry—that all a society needs is the instantly vanishing present of asignifying capital exchange. What arrogance! Yet as Bruno Schulz reminds us: "The word as a mosaic piece is a late product, an early result of technology. The primeval word was a shimmering aura circling around the sense of the world, was a great universal whole. The word in its common usage today is only a fragment, remnant of some former all embracing, integral mythology...The mythologizing of the world is not over yet; the process was only halted by the development of *scientia*, diverted into a side channel where it courses on without understanding its identity. But science, too, only fabricates its own world myth because myth is embodied in the very elements themselves, and there is no way of going beyond myth."

Bruno Schulz is correct: "There is no going beyond myth." That is why no work of art stands in isolation—not even in relation to other religions, philosophical systems, or mythologies 'outside' its own cultural and historical framework. *The Divine Comedy*, a work of western literature, has infinite connections with, for example, Taoist conceptions of reality, with Hindu ideas of the difference between knowledge and wisdom, with Judaic cosmologies, with the Kabbalah, etc., etc. And that is fitting, for in the end, as trivial and as 'corny', as it may sound, we are all one (in the very many that we are). The questions raised by one religion are the questions raised by all religions; the human problems addressed in Greco-Roman mythology, for instance, are found in all the mythologies of the world: from north to south, from east to west. The geography of humanity is universal. Whether we turn for guidance to Zeus or Krishna, Abraham or Mohammed, Buddha or Jesus Christ, it is not very important. What is important—what gives our lives meaning, is our 'meaningless' and pathetic Sisyphusean quest for answers that continue to escape our grasp.

"The thing that hath been, it is that which shall be; and that which is done is that which shall be done: and there is no new thing under the sun," writes the author of *Ecclesiastes* (1:9). That is why the great works of literature, written thousands of years ago, remain as alive today as when they were first written. The questions concerning the human condition are eternal and unanswerable, and no amount of technology— "not even" the Internet, is going to provide us with the answers once and for all. The ways to enlightenment are basically the same in every religion. It is Love (the unifying quality of consciousness) that leads us there. It is Hate (the separating quality of self-consciousness and desire), which leads us to war, oppression, poverty, and all kinds of social disharmony. And it is up to any culture worthy of its name to engage itself in a constant process of remembrance, while creating new myths from the old ones.

I wrote *The Electric Comedy* out of ignorance, and in so doing I learned how ignorant I was, and how ignorant I am, after having learned so much. One of the most important things lacking in American society—perhaps because it is so young, is true humility. Humility before the universe and humility before our masters, those who have so much to teach us. Carrying the torch of democracy, we may some day wipe out the whole of humanity and the natural world because we don't believe in masters or mastery, and are narcissistically willing, like the Greek god, Phaethon, to take on the responsibility of leading a chariot that we do not know how to drive. Like Phaethon, if we are not stopped, we are bound to burn the world down, with all the information and scientific knowledge (*scientia*) we lack the wisdom (*sapienza*) to understand.

Not being very good at much of anything, except for perhaps writing, this book is my own way—humble as it is, to save some very fine things from disappearing from that sphere of reality we once called the 'human'. If anything, I hope you like *The Electric Comedy* so that it sends you back to Dante, Virgil, Homer, Plato, *The Old Testament, The New Testament, The Koran, The Bhagavad Gita, Tao Te Ching, The Epic of Gilgamesh*...to ask the kinds of questions that may save us in the end.

I have left some blank lined pages at the end of each section of *The Electric Comedy*, so that you may begin, if you so wish, to write your 'own' comedy, your 'own' epic, or whatever else inspires you to create new myths for living a deeper and more meaningful life in this culture, and for the future.

Rolando Perez
Franklin Square, NY
May 7, 2000

Contents

Preface
Pages vii-xii

INFERNO
Pages 1-83
Reader's/Writer's Canto
Pages 84-86

Purgatorio
Pages 87-93
Reader's/Writer's Canto
Pages 94-96

PARADISO
Pages 97-110
Reader's/Writer's Canto
Pages 111-113

INFERNO Revisited
Pages 114-116

NOTES/GLOSSARY
Pages 117-146

List of Illustrations
Page 147

> *Our hearts know no weariness because they are fed with fire, hatred, and speed!.. Erect on the summit of the world, once again we hurl defiance at the stars!*
> —Marinetti, 1911

INFERNO

> *Twenty five great powers govern the world, fighting over the markets of a superabundant industrial production. And this is why we finally arrive at the first electric war.*
> —Marinetti, 1914

2

Canto 1 (36)

In the beginning was the flesh,
and the flesh became word,
and the word became memory,
and our memory became electric.
Then in a puff of smoke,
gone was the age of the Ancestors,
gone was the age of History.
The exteriors all changed.
The desert, the arctic,
and everything in between disappeared—
or more accurately, reappeared as something other.
Something few of us had ever seen;
a brave new world,
born of a bloodless womb.
Some of us—the brave ones—got
on our vehicles and set out
to explore the new world:
hoping to find the promised signs of a new life.
But when we got there,
there was nothing.
A deception, a lie:
the interior had not changed at all.
Disappointed,

4

some of us returned
blinded by artificial stars, and worse,
some of us did not return at all:
trapped in a web,
impossible to escape.
And yet most of the inhabitants
here believe that this is the best
of all possible worlds:
safe, clean, secure, and ethical.
But where is the blood?
Where is the body?
And this thing of an "artificial mind,"
what could this possibly be?
Anyone who has studied philosophy
knows that a virtual substance
is a contradiction in terms.
"Yes, but as everyone here knows,
thanks to electricity
the ARTIFICIAL becomes the REAL,"
I am reminded by an eager young man,
full of potential,
lacking in qualities.
Thus our dreams, our nightmares,
our longings, and our desires
have become electric, subtle,
even transparent.

No more chains,
no more pulleys...
but electric pulses
transferred at excessive speeds
by our "new and improved"
desiring machines.

CODA:

    There would be no use in repeating all that Thamus said to Theuth in praise or blame of the various arts. But when they came to letters, This, said Theuth, will make the Egyptians wiser and give them better memories; for this is the cure of forgetfulness and of folly. Thamus replied: O most ingenious Theuth, he who has the gift of invention is not always the best judge of the utility or inutility of his invention to the users of them...for this invention of yours will create forgetfulness in the learners' souls, because they will not use their memories; they will trust to the external written characters and not remember of them-selves. You have found a specific not for memory but for reminiscence, and you give your disciples only the pretense of wisdom; they will be hearers of many things and will have learned nothing; they will appear to be omniscient and will generally know nothing; they will be tiresome, having the reputation for knowledge without the reality.

                                      — Plato
                                  Socrates in *Phaedrus*

Canto 2

The great divine Dante had Virgil
to guide him on his journey.
I, on the other hand, had no one,
except for few old maps
left behind
by my mentor,
my teacher and friend,
the courageous rope walker,
the courageous Captain N.
The old skipper
could not have imagined
for even a second,
how cold, how chilly,
the seas would become.
The ape is no longer
a painful embarrassment,
an object of shame to man.
For this other idea of someone greater,
is today's joke
taught to school children
correctly seated
before their screens: watching
their rich and famous

business heroes,
Nitel and Bim,
Tiny and Soft,
pixelated Supermen.

CODA:
    For matter to have so much power, it must contain a spirit. The souls of the gods are attached to their images...
                           —Gustave Flaubert,
                           The Temptation of St. Antony

Canto 3

It is always day here,
perpetually light and noisy
populated with billions
of desiring machines—
or as we also call them—
SUMERCONS,
who eat up everything.
These thirsty, propagating creatures,
are extremely dangerous
to those of us of the TISTAR tribes.
We are simply not as ferocious,

or as cunning, or as fast as they are.
Through Lack they were created,
and through Lack they exist,
hungry, thirsty
holes needing to be filled.
These SUMERCONS (or YAHOOS)
have developed
through some kind of de-evolutionary process
a rate of absorption
unequaled in recent history.
Even the most obscure TISTAR
can one day unexpectedly
find himself as another serving
on the dinner table of the YAHOOS.
Given the right, well-chosen
delectable images, on any monitor,
at any time, anyone can name
a rose whatever they desire. And though
TISTARS have endured,
like Saint Antony,
turning their backs
on all kinds of temptations,
their numbers seem to be dwindling,
and the world the SUMERCONS call
their 'heaven' is the world,
we the ungrateful,

the ones on the Left bank,
have come to call our HELL.

Canto 4

Arachne is not to blame.
It was not her, but us alone
who weaved
the web we're now entangled in.
A process began many
years ago when our breath was
turned to stone and we—in turn—could own it.
Then a big, clunky machine, with the help of trees
softened it: and our frozen breath became
an object of worship.
Ever since—the story goes—we've been
approaching invisibility,
flying off into space,
boundless, nameless, weightless,
far, far from the Earth
like bodies without organs
without a place to rest.
Pure energy without reserve,
speedily moving along virtual lines of flight,

the TISTARS believe the
planet is headed straight down into
a black hole,
existing in the curved,
nonlinear space of the profitable web
where our children today project their dreams of
the eternal NOW
for a few unimportant seconds.
The old GOD died in 1987,
a sudden, unexpected death for many
taking the horizon with him,
leaving behind the uncertainty
of a very complicated NET
and a web so very thin that one could easily
get trapped in it,
and there die, like one of those flies
at the marketplace, greedily flying
from place to place:
desiring to own and taste everything
NOW and at the same TIME.
Our SUMERCONS are the sons and daughters
of Phaethon.
Lacking the necessary knowledge
of their Ancestors,
they will turn the Earth to ashes,
and in the end will learn nothing from it.

For wisdom and information are
two very different things,
and those who cannot ride horses
should not ride them at all.

CODA:
    Phaethon, our god, is the father of DEINOS, god of electricity; born from the fire of Phaethon's chariot. It is to DEINOS that the SUMERCONS owe almost everything they have: from their net worth to all kinds of wonderful prosthetic devices specifically designed to make their lives' journey easier to navigate. It was DEINOS, the god of artificial light, who offered up the Elephant, in the name of his most holy mission on earth. Done, no doubt, as everything else in the Inferno, in the name of humanity.

Canto 5

The silence approaches.
She feels some pain,
and fearing that she will never see
her loved ones again, she cries
in the shadows of a rainy day.
All those years, minutes, seconds...
And from now on—Yes—No more future,
no more plans...just memories
of things that were

and some that may have been.
Everything slipping, slowly, slipping away.
"I can't hear," she says.
Her voice trembles with emotion,
and holding my hand in hers
I feel her pleading words:
"please don't leave, please don't leave...
I may never see you again."
But silence arrives nevertheless.
The whiteness, the darkness.
I don't know.
The alchemist doesn't know.
In the end, none of us know.
Leery as we may be of life
a projection of death
is just a projection.
This is not a death.
Timothy forgot that
and died alone
in the presence of millions:
consumed from within,
consumed from without.
The perfect SUMERCON death.
But neither love nor the brilliant glare,
the nice shiny surfaces,
the accumulation of bits

can keep the silence away.
In fact, the greater the number
of bits in our bank,
the greater the number of cells
in our blood, and everyone knows
what this means.
For though we attempt
to turn the old God's copper
into gold, an old decrepit worm
cautiously guards
our bodies:
the viruses to come,
and the gates to
the little infernos of our souls.

Canto 6

Time becomes visible—
all too visible to bear,
and heroically, in our own way,
we take the full weight of things
upon our melting shoulders,
leaving no space between A and B:

writing and reading archives
left behind by others just like us...
who took the world upon
their strong imagined shoulders,
called quicksand 'solid,' and
very much like Sisyphus
filled all the nooks and all the crannies
with invented plastic minutes.
But when everything was left unsaid
and everything was left undone—
and here is the moral of the story—
there really was no difference
between us TISTARS and the rest.
All pathetic little creatures
filling up their pathetic little holes,
leaving pathetic little markings,
digitally killing time.

CODA:
    Most TISTARS, due to their high degree of consciousness, feel a certain kinship with Sisyphus.

Canto 7

King Wilhelm opened the flood gates
of our polymorphous flows of desire.
His contribution: to release the appetites
from the clutches of gravity.
This metamorphosis began
over five hundred years ago,
when desire was discovered
to flow much easier over sea than land.
The sea could move in an infinite number
of directions, smoothly and fluidly.
Thus fittingly the great change began in a city
already half-submerged in water:
beautiful, sensuous, seductive, erotic—
open to all the exchanges of
desirable intercourse.
It would take half a millennium
for territories to completely disappear,
that is to say, to move from land to sea,
from sea to air,
from air to electricity.
A metaphysics of becoming...
becoming-atom, becoming-micro,
becoming-molecular,

arrived at through the use of energy
and wires. With this disappeared
the Captains of industry,
everyone now
captain of his own vessel.
The Reformation of KAPITAL,
could never have been imagined by
the bearded Jew and his sidekick
(not the actor and his brothers),
though we often confuse the two,
and treat the former as
the comics who misunderstood
the great Comedy of errors.
However, in their defense I should mention
that they are as young today
as they were one hundred and fifty years ago.
Perhaps even more so.
It's just that King Wilhelm opened the flood gates,
and allowed the children to play with matches,
and a lenient king is always more popular.
Everyone can play as much as they want
with fire and electricity.
Of course, some of his subjects thrive,
the ones with a safety net
some of them survive,
and some of them die in a web

dreaming of their promised freedom.
But what matters
to the King is his subjects' flows of desire
passing softly through his gates.

Canto 8

This is but a brief moment in the life of a man and a woman who were born in a cave, and have never left it. The names they gave themselves are XXApPLS4U (woman) and GnxDYsr4U (man).

XXApPLS4U: That's going to cost you $150 for 15 minutes.
GnxDYsr4U: Very well.
XxApPLS4U (putting on her visor): Are you ready?
GnxDYsr4U (putting on his visor): Yes.
Three thousand miles away.
He extends his hands,
touches nothing,
an image.
He runs his hands through a 'body'
somewhere else in space...
"probing....probing....feeling..."
every inch of her 'flesh'...

slowly with his fingertips...
gently caressing her 'breasts'...
bringing his 'mouth' closer, ever closer...
encircling her 'nipples' with his 'lips'...
running his 'tongue' around their 'tips'.

She responds digitally,
fleshly he imagines.
She opens her 'legs'....takes his 'hand'
and brings it to her 'pussy':
"dripping wet" she says.
He 'feels' her 'wetness'
three thousand miles away.
"You are so wet," he says.
Wet. She grabs his 'cock,'
and says "You are so hard."
Hard. "I want you to put it inside me."
Inside. Inside me.
"I'm going to put my cock inside you," he says
three thousand miles away.
$40.00 left
Inside you.
She guides his 'cock' inside her 'pussy'.
Inside her.
Three thousand miles away.
He can feel his "cock inside her".
And he's "thrusting...in and out..."

"It feels so good," she says.
"Oh, yes, you're so wet...
I'm going to cum..."
"Cum for me, baby, cum..."
01:30 minutes left.
$7.00 left.
Three thousand miles away.

He can feel his excitement
electronically...in the way
she responds to the impulses
of a soul bought and paid for
with the sacred currency
one has and does not have.
He grabs her 'ass' tightly
and then no longer able
to contain the 'friction'
of a frictionless universe
with $0.75 left,
he "cums inside her"
0:00 minutes left
on his temporary visa.

GNXDYSR4U: Ahhh!
XxApPLS4U: That's it.

He removes his visor and so does she
in their airconditioned caves
three thousand miles away.

Canto 8 1/2

Lights! Cameras! Action!
He tries to conjure up some images
as she lies in bed
at night bringing his hand lower
closing her eyes
touching ever so gently...
attempting to bring himself
into her image,
into his body as she moves
her hand with him...
but nothing happens.
Something is not working...
not bringing it off.
He places the dark plastic case
into a black box
and she begins again...
this time much better.
Images flickering...
her hand moving faster...
her fingers caressing
himself as he feels her
excitement...coinciding
with the predigested electric

images of the deathly black box.
Ah...ah...ah...*petite mort*
of that most dangerous supplement.
The hand rests, the fingers flex.
Someday he won't be able
to do this anymore
without the aid of
a *magic* box before him,
as Thamus had already predicted.
Oh, my sweetest, lovely Duclinea
I see you coldly replaced
by so many external projections.
And there begins the tragedy
of the simulacra as the real.
Ojo!: un altro film senza speranza.

CODA:

    Nine times the heaven of the light had revolved in its own movement since my birth and had almost returned to the same point when the woman whom my mind beholds in glory first appeared before my eyes.

—Dante Alighieri
La Vita Nuova

Canto 9

The greatest nightmare
facing TISTARS today
is the coming of the drought.
Some of us have already faced
the first pangs of an unquenchable thirst:
made yet more infernal
by an electric cold front
that will not go away.
As in Flatland, our neighbors,
our geometry has changed:
our lines have become thinner,
indistinguishable,
much more difficult to read
without the aid of transformers
that change them into images.

This one-dimensional world
without trees, children,
camels, or lions, is the world
of the YAHOOS and the SUMERCONS,
the world of the RESMANIAC.
These bloodless creatures
seem to exist—to subsist even—
on a daily diet of electricity,

deriving their nutrients
from high speed, semi-conducting units.
And so everything the RESMANIAC do
is hollow, and lacking possible
human greatness.
For since they have no rational organ
by which to distinguish what is bad
from what is great,
their heroes often die alone and destitute,
homeless in the streets of Baltimore.

But, one must admit,
the RESMANIAC are entertaining.
No one can deny them that.
They have devoted a great deal of time
and effort to this profitable enterprise.
So entertaining, that even their last war,
the one fought over the fuel
turned out to be nothing more
than an electronic game
produced & directed by a toy manufacturer.
But make no mistake about it,
the war did take place—
we know,
and Pinocchio's nose did grow
with all that devastation.

24

And as they say, or don't say,
but is most likely said for them:
As long as their blue velvet lawns
remain sparkling green
in the artificial horizon
of their neon dreams,
they have what they call 'freedom'—
a contradiction in terms.

CODA:

    My master continuing his discourse said, there was nothing that rendered the Yahoos more odious than their undistinguishing appetite to devour everything that came in their way, whether herbs, roots, berries, the corrupted flesh of animals, or all mingled together; and it was peculiar in their temper that they were fonder of what they could get by rapine or stealth at a greater distance than much better food provided for them at home. If their prey held out, they would eat till they were ready to burst, after which nature had pointed out to them a certain root that gave them a general evacuation.

    —Jonathan Swift,
    "Voyage to the Houyhnhnms"
    Gulliver's Travels

Canto 10

What is the meaning of life?
Why is there something rather than nothing?
Why is the world made of water?
Why can't you step into the same river twice?

These silly, old questions
echo through the leaning tower of knowledge:
vast and empty these days.
You want an answer?
You don't need the tower for that.
An engine named
after the hated YAHOOS of yesterday,
will help you navigate
and swallow the bits,
fast and easy like soup.
Search: MEANING AND LIFE
Search: SOMETHING AND NOTHING
Search: WORLD AND WATER
Search: RIVER AND TWICE

In nanoseconds
the most recent results
come up first!

The newest! The very latest!!!
One need not get lost in
the labyrinthian halls of
the old tower with all those
arborescent dusty scribbles
when the *Scientia* of the rhizomes
is so much easier to digest.
The complex logic of A AND B
makes it possible for anyone
to see the questions on a screen.
No need to think of it:
the created natures slew Minerva
not so long ago.
Dante, for instance, had to undergo a journey,
but that's because he lacked an engine
named after his guide.
Today with VIRGILIO.IT
he could Search: SIN <u>AND</u> REDEMPTION.
And presto! The time he could have saved!

What is the meaning of life?

Canto 11

I speak.
I utter a sound.
No response.
Not from SUMERCONS, not from TISTARS,
not from the UTILSS OF LISTEAR.
No response from anyone at all.
I throw a stone to sound out
the depths of an abyss
that is not even shallow.
I speak.
No one responds.
I extend my hand in a pathetic attempt,
but there is no one here
to acknowledge the Fall,
the vacant call of the wild
coming from the THIRD WORLD.
The last inhabitants left
many years ago
in search of a City of white light
in the valleys of the FIRST WORLD.
Inspired by an artificial sun
too bright,
and an artificial sound
too loud,

they disappeared in the glare
of a transistorized,
western, electric,
deterritorialized nightmare.
The transmissions, they explained, were not
for everyone to make.
Certainly not for those living
in the territorial margins
of the world: in grass huts and mud floors.
And so obeying the Libertarian Laws
of King Wilhelm
they closed their gates and windows
to every wanderer of pain,
hope, and happiness as well.
"No time, no time," they said.
"We're running."
Correre a la morte.
"We already gave.
At last, at last, everyone is free
to create his own kingdom!"
Yes, I can see your enthusiasm,
your positive attitude,
and a positive attitude is everything,
but does anyone
have any idea who that emaciated soul
outside the door

in the empty, cold snow, belongs to?
Does anyone? Does anyone care?
For it is not kingdoms she desires.
What she needs is a little more basic.

No response.
No transmission.
The gates and windows are all closed.
And yet they tell me "don't despair".

CODA:
    The warmth of a piece of iron or wood is in our opinion more impassioned than the smile or tears of a woman.
—Marinetti
Selected Writings

Canto 12

Thousands of miles away,
"and not far from here"
a savage runs across a field
carrying a spear in hand.
"He throws the spear, he kills a deer,
takes it home, and cooks it
for dinner...in a primitive stove,"
invented 50,000 years ago

before microwaves.
But wait! I see an airplane
crossing the sky from left to right
above the frame...a camera lens,
a microphone, some lights, some wires...
and the movement of the savage
is only real
far from the "exotic lands"
of national geographies...
beyond the shots, beyond the frame,
beyond the image of a telephoto lens.
So where is the savage?
Where has he run to? Where is his deer?
Where is his dinner? Where is his family?
Where is his feast
beyond the western circuitry?
Who made him up?
The entertaining RESMANIAC perhaps?
We have traveled millions of miles—maybe
even billions—sitting in front
of our electric magic boxes.
But we haven't sweated,
we haven't hunted, we haven't built a
hut we can call our own—or even seen
anyone build one (least of all a savage),
physically in front of us, for that matter.

All to cool, all too unreal,
we sometimes forget that representation
is not "rule by presence"
but rather dominion by absence.
And the pixelated savage has not
extended our central nervous system
past a minimal distance of 4 or 5 feet.
In the end nothing remains of Africa
at thirty second intervals.

CODA:

    That neither our thoughts, nor passions, nor ideas formed by the imagination, exist without the mind, is what every body will allow. And to me it seems no less evident that the various sensations or ideas imprinted on the Sense, however blended or combined together (that is, whatever objects they compose), cannot exist otherwise than in a mind perceiving them...Their *esse* is *percipi*, nor is it possible that they should have any existence out of the minds or thinking things which perceive them.

                      —George Berkeley
                    Part I, Of the Principles of Human Knowledge

Canto 13

The journey in the ancient Republic
took place from the exterior of the country
(from the molar)
to the interior
(to the molecular).
And though our destination is different,
the journey has changed very little.
Confusing a lexicon with reality
it was easy for Power to lose the argument.
Moreover, the City of light
was not the one
favored by he
who came down from the mountain.
Someone else—a very hungry scholar—
called the fair city
a "city of pigs," and demanded
Plutus' city:
Our City of SUMERCONS and YAHOOS.
And so today everything is exchanged
from love to the latest stocks
in the marketplace of 'Ideas'.
Molar examples:
Soap, detergent, underwear, hammers,

coffee, pork bellies, oil, and beans.
And falling somewhere in between,
like products at the supermarket
issues are displayed
on the same shelves advertising:
abortion, gun control, smoking,
health insurance, business ethics.
Here today, gone tomorrow:
replaced by new and improved
and exciting things: Y2K or K-Y Jelly.
It's all the same.
The molecular examples are just
as many: the restless bees that lay their honey
like in that infamous allegory
of the beehive
where avarice is everything,
and love can only slow you down.
But what if the coupling between the bees,
between our desiring machines, went wrong;
and due to stress the bees failed to couple?
What then? What would that say
for speed and electricity?
The SUMERCONS have an answer ready for that.
It is an electrical, chemical answer.
An artificial desire enhancer
solves the immediate problem,

even if in the end
all you're left with is
some kind of twisted love...
with some arousal.
But what if the chemical 'answer' fails?
Not to worry.
The City has planned for it:
the chemists—not the philosophers—
will turn the switches off
and make everyone
feel happy about it.

CODA:

    Antibiotics, computers, and, in general terms, all ultramodern technology, including television, come under Pluto's sway...When first sighted in January 1930, Pluto was in the sign of Cancer, which traditionally rules China. We are at present watching the birth of a typically Plutonian civilization in what has become the third great world-power, its outlines emerging since about 1971....In analytic astrology, Pluto [the Master calls him *Dis*] is the Prince of Darkness, symbol of the depths of our inner darkness which is linked to the primordial night of the soul...

—Jean Chavalier & Alain Gheerbrant
Dictionary of Symbols

Canto 14

Busy reader
I understand how little time you have
for yourself, for your friends,
and for your family.
Ever since we cleverly invented
a way by which to keep track of time—
as though that were ultimately possible—
we have been chasing
either a shadow on the ground,
or numbers on a dial.
And all throughout that short history
we have been made promises
that the shadow we're chasing will
someday very soon slow down for us,
as though the shadow and the numbers
could exist without us.
But the shadow—now digital—
has not slowed down,
but rather has speeded up
with the wonders of electricity.
Desiring-production is the manna of
Chronos—the only god left to worship—
who constantly eats his children.

So if you could give me a few moments
out of your busy schedule
and turn off your mobile 'communicators,'
and your electric magic boxes,
I promise I will be brief,
for as you can see thus far
my Comedy is concise,
but it does require a little 'thinking'.
I know, I know, such words these days
bring out a smile…
occasionally some laughter.
But then "one must be a buffoon
to be a philosopher," said Captain N
in the days before the wires.
If that was true then,
it is even more so now:
in the age of our virtual 'democracy'
where everyone is equal—
equally tired.

One hundred years ago
some enemies of the 'laborsaving' machine
took to the factories
with hammers and picks
because they wanted a little more time
to play.

Busy—like you—they saw the replacement
of the soul with desiring-production,
and wanted to bring that system down.
Nothing funny about it;
for there is nothing as serious
as the spirit of play.
Our children today
have forgotten all about it,
and these enemies of *technolopoly*
are portrayed as ridiculous,
"enemies of the people"
in thirty seconds or less.
The River Lethe runs past

the house of every child:
this is the water they drink,
and the river they forget as they drink it.
I'm sorry, I'm beginning to feel that

I'm losing you, that I'm boring you,
that I have gone on too long.
Please don't let me keep you,
I will end it here,
so you can turn everything back on—
if you hadn't already done so
(and were reading these words
at the same time you were doing
so many other important things).
Least important of course,
the words of a buffoon
fighting 'imaginary' windmills.
For what is the usefulness of that
when the wired and the wireless
are here to stay?
"You are a Luddite,"
they say,
and continue changing channels.

Canto 15

"Either it exists NOW or
it doesn't exist at all."
Whatever exceeded one hundred years
the SUMERCONS quickly erased;
replaced the Harrow
with a brand new machine
not to preserve our memories,
but rather to destroy them.
And so the bloody inscriptions
of the men-in black,
gave way to the bloodless images
of the men-in-white,
images that lasted no more
than a few seconds
in the micro-cerebral cortex.
One no longer had to write:
HONOR THY SUPERIORS.
Finally civilized
we see evil shadows in the cave
of "someone else's" penal colony.
It's not our bodies on the wall.
Torture ended long ago,
with the death of ideology.

Hocus pocus, Locus-Solus.
Everyone his own slave,
everyone his own master,
oppressed oppressor oppressed:
free at last, free at last!
We are the Harrow, we are Bim,
we are all the machines
in history.

CODA:

    I, this 'I', sees the tree and asserts that 'Here' is a tree; but another 'I' sees the house and maintains that 'Here' is not a tree but a house instead. Both truths have the same authentication, viz. the immediacy of seeing... What does not disappear in all this is the 'I' as universal whose seeing...is a simple seeing,...When I say 'this Here,' 'this' 'Now', or a 'single item', I am saying all Thises, Heres, Nows, all single items. Similarly when I say 'I', this singular 'I', I say in general all 'Is'; everyone is what I say, everyone is 'I', this singular 'I'.

                                              —G.W.F. Hegel
                                              Phenomenology of Spirit

Canto 16

The UTILSS OF LISTEAR
are excellent marksmen.
With bow and arrow they take aim,
and hit only at the center.
If the target seems too distant,
and there is no prize
in hitting it,
like children at a luna park,
they move on
to more profitable amusements.
For instance, enemy of the Muses,
they love the electric theater.
Fast moving in a well-defined,
if contrived direction,
the end always comes
beautifully wrapped
like stuffed little animals
made of straw.
The RESMANIAC invention:
to make each scene
of the electric theater
only important for the next one.
What you saw is what you saw.

42

In the eclipse of an adventure:
if you make it count, you make it boring,
and as the UTILSS OF LISTEAR know,
the most useful place in a house
is the restroom.

CODA:
> We shape clay into a pot
> but it is the emptiness inside
> that holds whatever we want.
> —Lao-tzu
> *Tao Te Ching*

Canto 17

A bloodied razor glistens.
"It wasn't my fault,
it was the sun."
And once again the excuses
for acts too horrible to forgive
even at the beach,
sitting beneath umbrellas
comfortably drinking margaritas.
There is no good
and there is no evil here,
now that everything weighs equally

in our comfortable POST-inferno.
Drop a feather, drop a rock,
they hit the ground at the same time.
Cold and scientific,
everyone an expert
with countless syllogistic reasons.
A bloodied razor glistens.
But the master did not
flinch when they put his fellow humans
in the belly of the Sicilian bull
and set the 'bull' on fire.
A far worse sin it was for him
to steal from the sacristy,
or to have a little pleasure,
pleasurably from behind.
The horror, the horror,
the cruelty & the spectacle,
a surplus value of pleasure.
But nothing can justify the knife
which cuts the human heart...
hiding behind an image.
Who in this land can honestly demand
even a shadow of love
when the bright fountains of evil
are constantly overflowing?
A bloodied razor glistens.
Everyone in a nice little box,

painted with many colors,
but for this they'll have to pay
a price, if not with their lives,
with their dignity.
Such was the birth of a ('free') nation,
such was the birth of the fountains of evil.
A bloodied razor glistens.
Ten million people died...
Ten million people died... .
Ten million people died...
Ten million people died...
Ten million people died...
Ten million people died...
Ten million people died...
...in the camps...
...in the camps...
...in the camps...
...in the camps...
...in the camps...
...in the camps...
...in the camps...
Copy and paste a history.
We must never forget
the difference between
shoabusiness and people.
I'm very sorry Captain N,

but good and bad are not enough.
All great cultures need more than that—
their tables and their scales.
Besides, to quote you now,
(my own guide, my own 'Virgilio'):
one repays one's teacher badly
if one remains only a student;
and the same goes for the two Frenchmen
who once attempted to kill
the guilty man afraid of seeing.

Canto 18

First came the men in black
with their crosses,
then came the well-dressed men
with their guns,
and then came the men in white
with their wires.
And this is what happened:
the crosses were too big
and everyone could see
what it was that they were up to.

So having tried the crosses
and very badly failed
the second time they came
they returned with powder and explosives,
but the explosions were too loud
and that business also failed
(according to the *anthrapists*).

At last, the men in black
became the men in white
(the offsprings of Morning Strife),
and this time instead of bringing guns
they came with something better—
an invisible magic weapon
having none of the obvious problems of the
crosses and the guns.
Imported from the western cities
this new RESMANIAC magic
eventually wiped out the
huts and the villages:
like some carcinogenic substance:
replicating itself without limit,
to make way for the new temples of Bim,
and the other deities of the
electric markets.
This is the story of Prospero

for the Age of Brightness—our age,
the age of King Wilhelm of the Gates.
But of course, it's just a story.
Though perhaps I should tell you
that there are those who believe it,
and those who claim to have 'witnessed'
the ravaging of the white plague:
marching silently and unnoticed
into the very center of the western lands.
And according to these 'witnesses,'
or 'madmen'—whatever you want to call them,
we have already started
dying from it,
whimpering,
in our last attempt
to dance with 'death'.

CODA:

    The Vikings...were pirates, and piracy is the first stage of commerce. So true is this that from the end of the ninth century, when their raids ceased, they simply became merchants.

>—Henri Pirenne
>*Economic and Social History
>of Medieval Europe*

Canto 19

Phaethon the Splicer is our national god,
immature and ignorant,
out of control,
he is driven by arrogance
into areas he does not know.
Our RESMANIAC god takes pride
in splicing and combining
one beast with another
to create a third.
Proud of his power, seemingly limitless,
he does away with the seasons,
when he creates new fruits,
grains, and vegetables
ex nihilo;
and increases the growth
and resilience
of Ceres' corn of yesterday,
with the science of Monsanto.
And so it has recently
come to our attention,
that Phaethon and Narcissus are brothers.
For why stop with vegetables
and the lower beasts,
when one can easily engender natures

as perfect and as brilliant
as Phaethon himself—
by splicing a little here,
a little there,
from Gaia's stream of creation.
SUMERCON parents want perfect children:
Mozarts, Beethovens, Einsteins.
A Minotaur perhaps?
Half man, half animal, part objects.
Man becoming-animal, animal becoming-man.
What is wrong with that?
Phaethon, god of RESMANIAC creations,
was born of the Enlightenment,
and everyone knows how much progress
we have made with all that light.
But what does the future hold for us
who live only in the present?
In the past we turned to geomancers,
astrologers, and oracles for such answers.
We believed in the Fate
the gods themselves could not escape.
But then the terror began.
The wired servants of Phaethon
craftily devised their own plots
to replace the moons, the planets,
and the stars with their own

double-headed god,
created *in vitro*.
"From now on we will know
what terrible diseases
you have inherited,
what you will die of,
and when you will die.
Life has to be insured.
Nothing personal. So come along,
come along, nothing to be afraid of.
There is nothing like being informed,"
they said with heads turned backwards,
scratching furiously.
But perhaps one day
out of embarrassment
of his own hubris and impotence—
like Minos—Phaethon will have to have
his own version of the Labyrinth made,
to hide the monsters he created.
That is, of course,
if he doesn't repeat the past,
and turn the world to cinders.
And as we all know,
RESMANIAC culture
doesn't like history.
We slew Mnemosyne long ago.

If Phaethon is our god,
Lethe is our River.

CODA:

...the most disturbing biotech work has been done in agriculture and animal husbandry, and most of us have so lost touch with the land and waters and the origin of our food that this domain is nearly invisible to us, so the creation of hundreds of transgenic 'frankenspecies' (pigs with elephant or human genes, plants with fish genes, gene altered giant salmon, etc., etc.) eludes our attention...Animals with human genes can now be patented in the U.S. Whole humans cannot because the 13th Amendment prohibits slavery (though human DNA and cells can be). What about animal-human hybrids? Will corporations create armies of primates with human genes to perform menial and dangerous labor, for example?

— J.P. Harpiginies
The Double Helix Hubris

Canto 20

With its countless temples to Plutus
there is no uglier city
than Metropolis N.
Its sharp towers of glass,
penetrate the whores of Babylon:
the ones who take,
the ones who are taken.
Nothing but Energy—
inexhaustible from morn to night.
Something dies?
Death too is turned to fuel by Chaos.
No pain, no gain.
They run with their prosthetic
voices and ears
(given to them by DEINOS),
busily like bees
absorbed in their own flights
optimistically wondering what the next
N second will bring them.
The concerns are the same for the
richest and the poorest man.
The more they spend,
the more energy and wealth increases.

In either case, every day at 0900 hours
supersonic vehicles traverse a bustling universe
in the reiterated nightmare of the New Metropolis
while mothers of the THIRD WORLD attend
to the children of the wealthiest women,
too busy for the cradle and the spindle.
White and brown faces, the same,
emigrating, each according to his station:
leaving wives and children behind.
In the past, the Master told us,
they left Florence
for a better life in France.
Presently they leave their countries,
for the promise of a better life
in this Inferno.
To think that this is the origin
of the RESMANIAC,
that they've all come so far for this:
crossed deserts and oceans,
scaled mountains and walls,
to reach this concrete paradise,
only to die like YAHOOS,
like wild beasts in the cold!
Somewhere else things are much worse, I am told
But what can possibly be worse?
A tree? A field? A stream?

Is that really worse?
The THIRD WORLD, conveniently for us,
lacks the necessary Energy,
and it is this which drives the thirst
for all those material girls.
Forasteros, olvidados, bicycle thieves,
young, successful couples
stepping out of limousines
into mansions and *bodegas*,
doing anything to enter
the land they've come to call—
lost in a forest forever,
listening to their own Echo—
the land of their 'salvation'.

CODA:
    The city is loveliest when the sweet death racket begins. Her own life lived in defiance of nature, her electricity, her frigidaires, her soundproof walls....In the early evening, when the crowd is sprinkled with electricity, the whole city gets up on its hind legs and crashes the gates. In the stampede the abstract man falls apart, gray with self, spinning in the gutter of his deep loneliness.
    — Henry Miller
    Black Spring

Canto 21

Afraid to live
the YAHOOS surround themselves
with countless objects
of electricity.
Having no place to go,
or anyone to talk to:
cut off from family and friends,
they enter states of trance,
to escape the great infernal sadness.
The places they frequent
are markets without centers.
Not a place to sit,
not a place to congregate,
not a single public space:
from the mines to the caves,
individual cells
wrapped in dirty hospital sheets
made from the flesh of their loneliness.
This is the life of YAHOOS today,
the life they fight so dearly
to preserve.
'Life,' to call it something.
But I have never seen them living.
Their cities are made

from the blood of greed,
and their towns do not exist.
A certain number of streets
for vehicles
fitting in a grid,
is what they call their 'towns.'
But who can tell one YAHOO 'town'
from another,
the way one can tell
Cortona from Ravenna.
Nowhere else, but in RESMANIAC culture
is the word 'community' used more
often, and nowhere else
does it exist so little.
Bored of it all like Belacqua,
bored with their fascinating objects
of electricity,
bored with the electric games
of death & cyberspace
given to them by
their deadly boring parents
with nothing to do
in their virtually
non-existent towns,
once in a while,
the children of YAHOOS

take to their schools
and with more than a few shots
attempt to put some holes
in an emptiness
no one cares to see
and no one cares to hear,
except, perhaps as an eclipse,
an empty view of fear.

CODA:
    In the deepest sense of the words [medieval town planning]...was both functional and purposeful, for the functions that mattered most were those of significance to man's higher life.
    —Lewis Mumford
    The City in History

Canto 22

Holding a young girl down
with bloodied hands
a metal instrument
or the hitting of two stones together
the old women
cut\smash\mutilate
the young girl's pleasure center
in the name of timid men
and their traditions.
This is one of many examples
that should inspire
horror and revulsion,
should inspire revolutions.
But RESMANIAC culture, always moderate
engenders creatures
who like to sit on fences:
refusing to pass judgment.
And why not?
Long ago the YAHOOS became Wasps,
and the Wasps have always had it easy.
"Open minds," they boast,
because there is nothing in them.
"What do you believe in?"

"What is your religion?"
And so they strain and strain
in deep philosophical thought
as though I had asked them
to solve an impossible riddle.
At last, however, comes their answer,
after much deliberation
in unison:
"This is the land of RESMANIAC,
this is the land of the free,
where we can say what we wish
without fear of imprisonment."
"Yes, I understand all that,"
I said to them.
"But you haven't answered my question.
What do you believe in?
Do you not see anything wrong
with torturing that poor girl
in the name of the camel
(who even for us in the West
had to give way to the lion
and the lion in turn to the child?)"
"Everyone's entitled to his
or her opinion. Every opinion
is as good as another," they said
putting their hands in their pockets,

(like the Roman of the thorny crown)
doing whatever they could
not to soil them.
"Then what is your opinion?" I persisted.
Silence. A long pause and then:
"This is a free country," said one
indistinct 'individual'
avoiding to offend anyone.
Ten million or fifteen million or
two hundred million...
bodies piled on top of each other.
Auschwitz or Rwanda.
"It's all opinion."
"Is there anybody out there?"
I call out:
Is there anybody out there?
responds the echo.
And I notice that the creatures
I've been talking to are hollow,
virtual,
made of nothing,
signifying nothing,
empty chambers.
The Master placed them in Limbo.
I have placed them in POST-Inferno.
For it is not them who suffer,

but the rest of us
who hear the young girl screaming,
and the cold silence
of these bodies without organs.
Neither mommy, nor daddy, nor me,
nor anybody else to be found here.
Avoiding disgrace—or even praise,
they will go to their graves
happily being nothing—
completely undisturbed
by the horror, the horror,
the evil.

Canto 23

"Power is the greatest aphrodisiac,"
said one of our statesmen.
The strongest natures lead,
the weaker natures follow.
The Neros, the Borgias,
the Mussolinis, the Hitlers,
earthly monsters,
earthly empires.
Built stone by stone,

today wire by wire,
by little men
who could not lead
a flock of sheep,
but knew so well to follow.
Reactive forces,
SUMERCONS lacking fire
desire only
what is created for them.
Their ambition—
and they are ambitious—
is to ascend
flying on the wings of Geryon.
And so they flatter
their superiors,
picking up the crumbs
Geryon leaves behind,
making their noses brown
with the feces in their nails.
The recognition they seek
from a president or prince,
is the one Thomas More,
and the brave Susanna
turned their backs on:
choosing death,

or the wrath of elders,
over submission to a law
less than just,
less than heavenly.
Times were different.
But the world is still divided
into TISTARS and SUMERCONS:
those who create,
and those who don't,
and the little man,
is the most dangerous of all.
Like tenure in a university

guarded by those who cannot lead
and those who cannot read
who attempt to control
the art of those who do
with a silly carrot and a stick.
"Mr. Rothko, your colors do not match
the colors of our team.

Jump, jump, or caput."
A little threat,
but nothing more:
empty and meaningless
for the warrior
not afraid of venturing into unknown lands.

Buried, the little man
remains trapped
in the excrement of his own resentment.
And the poison he attempts
on the lives of us TISTARS,
is the poison
we creatively turn to breakfast.

Canto 24

Apollo was the Master's
guiding light in Paradise,
guiding him to the freedom
of God's Everlasting love in Beatrice.
But for BRUNO and his brothers,
Circe, not Apollo,
was the pilot of the (drunken) bark.
Humble son of Gaia, he sought

neither freedom nor the sun
on journey,
but the privilege to be
one of Circe's many servants.
And so according to BRUNO
la verace storia went like this:
He, along with the others,
(and even Eurylochus), were more
than eager to please,
to go down on their knees:
to worship Circe's honeyed feet.
If she turned them into swine,
it's because that is what they wanted:
To submit, to be trampled upon
by her feet, to submit to her power:
to feel the sweet feeling of surrender.
To be as close to Hesiod's
terrifying Earth—
as close to Nothingness, as possible.
And then one day Zeus
in swastika and military boots
split the town of Drohobycz in two
with his mighty lightning bolt.
And that was the beginning
of the end for BRUNO.
Zeus declared him an inferior,
unworthy of human love,

and the submissive TISTAR
became BRUNO THE DOG—
no longer the servant of Circe,
no longer the servant of Venus in
the Island of Cythera;
but rather the sniveling dog
of one of Zeus' guardian,
who kept him alive
on a ration of gruel and some bread
in exchange for some pictures.
From a military boot
to a small dainty foot,
to a high heel shoe,
how much of a distance?
BRUNO the TISTAR,
BRUNO the teacher,
all kinds of submissions,
all kinds of indignities.
And it all begins
at the very beginning:
from the smallest blows
of the voiceless child
to the greatest humiliations
over many years:
till one is too tired
to fight any longer
and readily submits,

at last, triumphantly like a roach,
to the threatening shoe
dangling dangerously above one.
Perhaps this is why
there are lot more BRUNOS
drowning in a sea of twisted love
than there are great captains and seers.
Like photosensitive children
with their surprising
sacred disease
born under the sign of Pisces,
I see the roaches running
away from the light
to worship the feet
that will end
the sweetest suffering.

CODA:
    ...in the citadel of the sky, where the rising curve attains its consummation, and the downward slope makes its beginning and holds the summit towards midway between orient and occident and holds the universe poised in the balance, here does the Cytherean claim her abode among the stars, placing in the very face of heaven, as it were, her beauteous features, wherewith she rules the affairs of men.... Certain it is that the goddess of Cythera changed herself into a fish when she plunged into the waters of Babylon...and she has implanted in the scaly Fishes the fires of her own passion.

                                  — Manilius
                                  Astronomica

Canto 25

Only one god is said
to have died thus far:
The god who claimed to
be the ONE, the exclusive
Unmoved Mover.
But these are only rumors.
Gods do not die
by the hands of mortals.
They disappear for a while
and return as something else.
One of the Guardians of Zeus
fooled his population
by claiming to have castrated
old, blind Plutus.
With signs and symbols of crosses,
with signs and symbols of goodness,
robbing the words of Iesu,
a man who really meant them,
he promised his people,
in the name of Libra,
to balance Plutus with Poverty,
and bring *Dike*, the god of Justice
to his island of BAKU.
But that is not what happened,

either because there were far too
many citizens with their heads
deep in the soft, warm sand,
comfortably dreaming,
or because they failed to
heed the oracle:
beware of the improvers of mankind.
In either case, *Horai*
never made it to the island.
And the bearded one merely
took Plutus for himself,
leaving Poverty to his people.
This led to a great exodus,
and to that condition
the Master so well knew,
the condition of Exile.
The reasons people leave
are always many:
the threat of violence,
the threat of death,
or even the constant fear
of being caught with a little
food not officially sanctioned
by the government that be.
For this one paid dearly then—
one pays dearly now:

with death, torture, or imprisonment.
Not to speak of the indignity
suffered by a child
made to watch the guardians
making fun of his mother's
undergarments in
the presence of his father.
And all in the name of
Utopia and the messianic
promises of a material gospel,
flawed like any other.
In the end, "not even"
the thespian father of the Church
(BRUNO's half-brother).
could bring this Tyrant down.
One of these children,
the one who writes this now,
left with many others—
never to return,
living in exile,
an isolated TISTAR,
in the land of electricity,
SUMERCONS and YAHOOS.
The final twist in the story
is that he, the child
who once refused

to applaud the colors
red and brown,
today refuses to applaud:
the color green of young Plutus
and his cronies,
in the wealthy land of his exile.
"Beware," said Captain N,
(always my guide in the Inferno),
"of the improvers of mankind."

CODA:
   ...Intimately connected with it [red] are the two most profound impulses—doing and suffering, freedom and tyranny—as so many red flags fluttering in the winds of the twentieth century go to show!
   ...For both the Ancient Romans and the Catholic Church, brown was the color of humility (humus, earth), a motive for some religious orders to wear brown....Sadists have a predilection for brown—for example Hitler's Brownshirts....

—Jean Chavalier & Alain Gheerbrant
Dictionary of Symbols

Canto 26

Let us speak of exile
once again, and, of those
who neither by want
nor by Tyranny
sought another land.
The exile of those
who did not fit in the matrix
of Plutus, Empire,
Progress and Logic.
Contrary to Dante's *Monarchia*
there is no god-given right
to dominion over others.
An old, dried up idea,
of one who believed in Order,
Unity, and the Center.
But those of us homeless—
"the old chestnuts":
Captain N, Samuel, and James
sought shelter instead
in the peripheries of a web,
in a place of our own making
away from the catastrophe.
And here, we, the lost ones

utterly alone with others
suffer a pain,
sharp and unnameable,
in a silent universe
that no one but ourselves
are able to visit.
Perhaps this is the price
we pay for our hubris,
the avalanche which swallows
even the strongest TISTAR.
This is what I have learned
from my contemporary masters—
exiles like myself,
in this centerless Inferno.
Sam taught me the arts,
and to him I am indebted.
He taught me how to hide,
behind translucent, graphic glass.
The weightlessness, the lessness,
the crystalline breath of zen,
the beauty of its simplicity:
to say in a word
what it take others
to say in volumes.
If I could only write
seven words the equivalent

of this quiet, gentle soul,
I could die and almost die happily,
having scratched some beauty
on the white, empty
surface of silence.
Sam in turn learned his craft—
insofar as that is possible—
from the one-eyed James of
dark mythologies.
His eloquently vulgar Mr. Bloom,
a Ulysses, on a voyage
from Dublin to Cythera:
made the English signs fly
like the Master with his Italian.
In other words, I should tell you,
this is not my story, but theirs.
They left their fatherland
to escape the sealing of a fate
so many before them had accepted
with crosses around their necks.
James was Sam's father,
and Sam in silent darkness
fathered me,
which makes James my grandfather—
these, my kindred spirits in exile.
And let us be clear about it,

no tell-tale will lead us back,
to the time before the Inferno.
On this drunken boat we go,
onward, onward, worstward ho!
not to Paradise but to nothingness
in our dangerously little bark
of selfness.

CODA:
    By the end of October 1940, Beckett was a member of the fledgling French Resistance.... 'I was fighting against the Germans, who were making life hell for my friends, and not for the French nation'...

    —Deidre Bair
    Samuel Beckett: A Biography

Canto 27

I see a little tree
in the middle of nowhere.
Bare, bare it is.
"Nature has forgotten us,"
says Hamm.
Correction, we've
forgotten Nature.
Talking, talking, talking...
the ancient Greek
placed Logos high above it,
and Marinetti seconded it,
singing the hymn of
the UTILSS OF LISTEAR.
Walden III is this:
Our sky no longer offers shelter,
the world is heating up
birds no longer fly
in the blackened wormwood air,
fish longer swim
in the blackened wormwood waters,
lions no longer roar
in the blackened wormwood land.
Entire forests burnt
for the sake of Metatron

and his recordings.
"Not to worry, there is so much,
there will never be an end to it,"
declare the SUMERCONS who
proceed to pour seven bowls
of bitterness onto the world.
The plague of 'unnatural' desire
they see as the punishment
of the Fire punishing the Log.
But somehow they miss
the fire shooting across
the sky, the fire they themselves
created from Hiroshima to Chernobyl—
reckless children of Phaethon.
So proud of our Reason,
at the age of five
we teach our well-fed children
to write
their own checks
while laughing at history.
Lesson: when the wall came down
not so long ago, the first thing
the repressed SUMERCONS of the east
did was to make a pilgrimage
to the temples of Plutus,

neglecting to visit family
and friends in all the
pixelated excitement.
The images spoke of a
world getting better.
No more Harrow that was true,
but what was the alternative?
The freedom to be a SUMERCON
like everybody else?
In the midst of their festivities,
they failed to noticed that
east and west had always worshiped
the same deity.

The Empire of RESMANIAC,
to last an eternity!
But what of the THIRD WORLD?
Where are they in the net?
They trade undeveloped lands
for a fashionably decent god,
and life in the new metropolis.
What more could they possibly
ask for?
One gets used to having this
and having that...always,

already there, ready to hand,
instantaneously, and the smallest
deprivations will some day lead
the SUMERCONS to cut
each others' throats,
and that of all their neighbors.
Our chateaus, our civilization,
our Inferno, built on the shores
of Babylon—or RESMANIAC,
comes down to this: I.
Occhi, occhi, occhi.
"I want this and this and this...
and the world..."
So what is one to do?
How is one to avoid the polymorphous
mine fields, when there are
so many deceptive oases?
The time has come when it's too late
to clean up everything,
to wipe away the slightest trace
of a white plague no one dares to
call it by its right name,
for fear of being called
an enemy of the people.
It's been some time since Roland
went to battle, and even longer

since Beowulf fought the great Grendel
in the lake—Time of the great gods,
monsters, and heroes.
Our battles are electric,
imperceptible, and all that one
can do is avoid the exposed wires
touching blackened water.

CODA:
    'Nothing is vanity: all in the name of science, onward!' cries
the modern Ecclesiastes, that is to say Everybody!

—Arthur Rimbaud
A Season in Hell

Canto 28

The birth of Humanity
involved one complete and
merciless movement,
separating soul from body,
in the first moment
of our painful history.
Of Adam there is his rib,
of Eve there is her mouth,
of Prometheus there is his liver,

and of Pandora there is her sex,
all pieces of us
scattered throughout
a thousand tales written.
For in the writing was the fall,
the greatest Vanity of all
to think the One replaced the many.
I am the first incision.
You are the deed completed.
And with these tiny little words
began the Inferno
from which not even the Master
could escape
separating *I* from *world*,
world from *I*
forever burning from inside.
Always wanting to know more,
this brother of Faust,
blinked in *Paradiso*
and Beatrice, as a punishment,
went away.
The Master had once 'betrayed' her
gazing at another mistress.
Nothing celestial in this
foolish play of jealousy.
Alcibiades never looked

more ridiculous than when
he was jealous of Socrates.
From *I* to *I want* is but a
step in the beginning
of the end.
Even YAHOOS understand
from ego only blood can flow.
Do not be fooled by the Master,
the Master was a trickster,
a book of vengeance is what he wrote,
not a book of love.
Of course, it takes one to know one.
The cantos of the *Inferno*
equal *les chants de Maldoror*.
Blake on Milton was on target:
all the Poets side with Satan.
No one cares for cuckoo clocks.
BRUNO wanted to be nothing;
Sam wanted silence;
Dante wanted faith;
and Marsyas,
the proud artist,
was flayed alive
by a jealous god
I have always hated.
And when the children

of RESMANIAC
drunk with Self
look to the heavens
the star that guides them
in their lonely bark
is the brightly shining,
Morning Star.

CODA:
    There will never be enduring peace unless and until human beings come to accept a philosophy of life more adequate to the cosmic and psychological facts than the insane idolatries of nationalism and the advertising man's apocalyptic faith in Progress towards a mechanized New Jerusalem.

—Aldous Huxley
"Introduction,"
Bhagavad-Gita

Canto_____

85

Purgatorio

for Michael Malinowski

Canto 29

[Enter Belacqua,
Bartelby's not
so distant cousin;
with his arms folded
around his knees,
he counts the crumbs
in Pandora's valise.
He says,
to himself of course,
"I am almost done,
and soon I will leave."
Soon...soon...soon....
He picks up one of the
crumbs and looks at it
for a very long time
and at last recognizes it,
having seen it
so many times before.
With Johnny Sims,
that RESMANIAC go-getter,

he waits for his ship to come in.
Spera, he says. S...pe...ra.
SPERA, the goddess of Purgatorio,
the goddess of all
SUMERCONS and YAHOOS.
For it is SPERA who gives
Plutus his shine,
applied like the wax
on an apple.
Belacqua, our neighbor,
like us, connected
all the wires
and soon he will go,
if he wants to,
pack up his bags,
and simply go
like any other shade
in the greyness
wherever he virtually
wants to.
This is what it means
to be totally free
in RESMANIAC,
success, success, success,
piece by piece,
the promise of a cool million

a little rest in the end
and a week's vacation
in 'Mexico,'
in the comfort
of a homeless home.
Anyway, who is to say
what is real
when "war is peace"
and love is hatred?
Only a shade in a state
of near putrefaction
(sorry for the old word),
could possibly claim that
one could be a nomad
simply by moving in place,
and that the dead
are really living
consuming in shopping centers.
Mmmmm....what a beautiful, shiny apple,
says Belacqua,
a fastidious fellow and all,
with respect to his colourful diet.
We like it, too.
And when SPERA extends her arm
with the apple in her hand
we, the other shades, take it,

so shiny, so tasty it seems,
we bite it:
so rotten, so bitter...
"But wait, tomorrow will be better."]

CODA:
    'When I put on the television, after a while there's the feeling that images are just pouring into me and there's nothing I'm able to do about them.'
                    —Jerry Mander
                    Four Arguments For The Elimination of Television

Canto 30

[TISTARS engulfed in greyness
take one step
then the next
producing no movement at all:
impotent to change
the color of the landscape.
'Fortunate' are the many,
who according to the Law
of Higher Numbers,
remain shadows of their desires
blind to their own

projections in a cave.
This is what Belacqua was
thinking when the Master came
upon him:
If one could only be, simply one
or simply other—that is to say,
simply slave or simply free,
how much easier life would be
in this capital of pain,
for the ones who find themselves
trapped, somewhere in the middle
of Zeno's paradoxical world.
Poor old Sisyphus is content,
just as long
as he remains,
a clown like any other
unconscious of his condition.
Having fought all the battles,
made the rounds of the 'town'
with Mr. Bloom and everybody:
knocked on all the doors,
and spoken to all the right people,
Belacqua is really tired,
and now wishes to retire
to a simulated world
in his nothingness suburbia

with his Dante and his mouse
click click clicking away.
Lost with nothing to do,
as Captain N predicted,
why not wish,
like humble BRUNO,
for the *materia prima*
of manikins,
or the virtual reality
of a totally exhausted nation?
Oh, my brother Captain N,
what's the use of climbing
when there is no longer up,
no longer down?
Sam's Belacqua remembers
the day,
grey it was,
grey it was,
when we dismantled
Jacob's ladder;
then thoughtlessly went on
to unchain Gaia
from the Sun.
Sedendo et quiescendo
The sedentary
Belacqua answers:

Nothing to be done.
Feeling vanquished,
no one cares either way.
The light so near,
the light so far,
betrays already a fallen star.]

———

CODA:
    Lemy Caution: Why does everyone look so sad and miserable [in Alphaville]?
    Natasha: Because they lack electrical energy.

—Jean-Luc Godard
Alphaville

Canto_____

I've seen nations rise and fall
I've heard their stories, heard them all
but love's the only engine of survival
—Leonard Cohen
The Future

PARADISO

If you dream alone, it's just a dream
If you dream together, it's reality.
—Brazilian Folk Song

Canto 31

It took millions of years
before the Earth was able
to give birth
to her children again.
And on the 7th day,
from the richest
and weary forest
of our odyssey,
there sprouted countless
beautiful flowers,
and the green of the greenest lands
beneath our longings
of things unnameable and loved.
Then early one Spring
during the gentlest month
of the year,
the month of our first truth,
the month of our first seeing,
the first POST-Inferno children
were born:
self-propelled as moving wheels
in their innocence of becoming...
they headed without fear into a clear

and infinite horizon without limit.
Our horizon, the horizon of all gods,
at last returned to us:
the weight of all things,
gravity, the orgiastic rituals,
the resurrected goddesses,
the myths and the religions.
SUMERCONS dead,
the YAHOOS dead,
the UTILSS OF LISTEAR dead,
RESMANIAC dead.
And that which once floated
without substance—virtually,
has finally taken shape.
Never a lion without qualities,
a body without fire.
Which is to say:
"This is good, this is evil.
This is true, this is false."
Nothing in the middle.
We remember Buddha, Krishna,
and the others.
No more walls to push
in the name of DIRTEC,
KAPITAL, and Plutus.
Pushing, pushing,

the YAHOOS were the first
to perish from the spiritual
hernias of their souls.
Der wille zur macht—
mere words, bad directions
from a journey gone wrong.
Nothing to overcome here,
nothing to conquer,
nothing to colonize,
nothing to prove,
no reason to utter
the imperial **I**
in a world which flows,
which sings,
which dances,
and loves.
"**I will**" is the return to hell,
we always say in our prayers.
In the innerlands of Paradiso
there are no illusions.
Our dancing stars
dance eastward
and no one cares to move "the walls";
for the walls are always moving
to the rhythm of our songs.

CODA:
>
> Water flows continually into the ocean
> But the ocean is never disturbed:
> Desire flows into the mind of the seer
> But he is never disturbed.
> The seer knows peace:
> The man who stirs up his own lusts
> Can never know peace.
> He knows peace who has forgotten desire.
> He lives without craving:
> free from ego, free from pride.
> This is the state of enlightenment in Brahman...
>
> —"The Yoga of Knowledge"
> *Bhagavad-Gita*

Canto 32

The Master in the *Inferno*—
in his *Paradiso* even,
was a man in hell.
Not wanting to embrace the many
a monarchy on earth he set;
by divine right, he said:
my Empire over the colonies,
the wolf over the lamb.
An idea that lasted a thousand years.

We on the other hand say:
we are, we do.
We know where Tantalus went wrong.
And that is all we know.
Harmony is piloted by Love:
who gathers everything together
and makes the world ordered Chaos.
Love here does not judge,
Love here does not exclude.
Hell is as much the One
as hell was once the Other.
Meaningless distinctions.
Words of a distant past:
bricks in the tower of Babel.
Not one god, but many—
as it really was for Dante—
rule in Paradiso.
"O buono Apollo,"
he invoked
on entering the Empyrean.
Beatrice noticed
and called him on it
on being torn by
one desire and the other.
For hell begins with **I**,
as hubris builds upon it,
giving birth

to Phaethon's fire
from within and from without.

CODA:
    At one time we shall descend, dismembering with titanic force the 'unity' of the 'many,' like the members of Osiris; at another time we shall ascend recollecting the same members, by the power of Phoebus, into their original unity.
                              —Giovanni Pico della Mirandola
                                  Oration on the Dignity of Man

Canto 33

Though not certain
when it happened,
in Dream Time
it could have been.
A thousand years ago,
in the Age of Electricity,
the Age of Simulacra;
also known
for the *white plague*:
suddenly one day
all the machines stopped—
from the black magic boxes
in every home
to Bim's and King Wilhelm's

"all powerful, all knowing"
desiring machines.
Plutus, unchecked by *Penia*
grew so big
that no one in the end
seemed to be able to
bring him down.
SUMERCONS and YAHOOS grew obese
beyond imaginable human proportions.
They devoured everything in sight
virtual and real,
declaring their "internal
contradictions"
not to be contradictions at all,
laughing at the oracles
of a bearded man:
who predicted
their great fall.
And just when gold would
never end
Midas' kingdom ate itself
and young Phaethon, by mistake,
burned the net
and burned the wires
of King Wilhelm of the Gates.
Down, down went RESMANIAC
down, down went the Empire.

Hocus-pocus! Magic pride!
Locus Solus,
gone is **I**.
Nature, Flesh, and Soul
together at last
we enjoy this Paradise.

CODA:

...there came a day when without the slightest warning, the entire communication system broke down, all over the world, and the world, as they understood it, ended....She had never known silence...the silence of the earth and of the generations who have gone...

...Ever since her birth she had been surrounded by the steady hum....

.... 'I am dying—but we touch, we talk, not through the Machine'.

He kissed her.

—E.M. Forster
The Machine Stops

Canto 34

Far, far, on the other side of Arcadia
when the night sky covers us
minute points of light
make their way from Metropolis
to remind us of our perished center:
the former devastations of forests,
air, seas, and natural energies—
our 'progressive' poisons.
But now imagine this:

Clear, crystalline brooks
gently flowing
from our emerald seas
into virgin, unpolluted rivers...
cool groves embracing us
with their foliage
welcoming us into them
while we take our place
at last beside our siblings
of land and sea:
the lions...the camels...
the sharks...the whales
as one, as many...
male, female, and as Marsilio

sung it: even the third sex...
before division...
we entwine our bodies like ivy...
ivy touching flesh...flesh to flesh
not as images
in black magic boxes...
bodies of flesh and bone...
conducting bodies of electricity
naked...pulsating with life...
pulsating with death
in a palpitating global village...
hands touching...
singing the body electric...
breast to breast...
breathing...
feeling the contours of our souls
and in this darkness a brightness
coming...coming...from nearby
...internal stars,
not from artificial lights...
sounds and vistas of a day
seemingly without end...
primeval forests...plateaus...
blue, open skies...
bluer than any blue before it
or after it...gasps...moaning

with infinite pleasure...
of human gods...daemons...
able to fly...without their wings
melting...without falling...
the wise Diotima with us...
in rainbows...in supernovas of Love...
Venus, Circe, Beatrice...

copulating...taking off...
in...in...faster...faster...
breathing pure air...
mouths, lips...moist walls...
as birds...absorbing one another...
caressing life...soul to soul...

soul to body and no split...
Apollo & Dionysus...
no seductive apples or trees...
no web...no net, unnecessary...
no dangerous supplement...
no 'I' to speak of...
the eyes see what is there...
not a place for RESMANIAC...
entangled with each other...
we mate with the world...
no vampire to stop us...
images of vampires...
in mirrors do not reflect...
only us...in the beginning...
the flesh, the soul, the same...
in the beginning was the end...
the rest a mediated lie at best...
the day we exchanged life for names...
and turned the living into death.

On four rivers we have traveled
with Marsilio in the stern
while Captain N
who knew a spider,
also knew our heavy bark
would one day sink...
again.

This birth, this death, our ship
he bravely named *amor fati*.
Oh, what a wonder it would be
to have Eros in our hearts
and when we looked up
to the sky
we could see
four dancing stars!

CODA:

    In the dusky streets around me ruled an open copulation. The entire town mated together, in the leafy bowers that had sprang up among the washing machines and the television sets.... Hundreds of couples of all ages caressed each other as they tried to teach themselves to fly...None of them was aware of their sex, as innocent as cherubs of what was taking place between them in these jungle bowers...I saw the bank manageress, standing with a peacock in her arms, offering money to the passers-by. Neither of them knew that they were naked.

—J.G Ballard
The Unlimited Dream Company

Canto_____

112

INFERNO Revisited

A struggle began for separation, for isolation, for personality, for mine and thine...They only vaguely remembered what they had lost, and they would not believe that they had ever been happy and innocent. They even laughed at the possibility of their former happiness and called it a dream...'The consciousness of happiness is higher than that of life, the knowledge of happiness is higher than happiness'—that is what we have to fight against.
      — Fyodor Dostoyevsky
        "The Dream of a Ridiculous Man"

Canto 35

For a very short time
everything was going well;
hell was far behind us.
We lived and loved in harmony.
always saying 'we'.
But then one day
a portly man came by
very hungry and very thirsty
and very angrily cried out:
"This is a city of pigs!
I want more,
I want wealth
I want the wires & the machines,
I want Logic
I want Reason,
long live Plutus!
I want the smoke I see
coming from the chimneys of Auschwitz,
I want you,
give me back my electricity,
give me back my shopping malls,
give me back the Berlin wall."
I am A (and you are not-A)

I have...
I will...
Cogito ergo inferno...
...again...
...again...
...again...
...again...
...again...
...again...
...again............................

I

CODA:
    What we call the beginning
    is often the end.
    And to make an end is to make a beginning.
    The end is where we start from...
                      —T.S. Eliot
                      "Little Gidding"

NOTES/GLOSSARY

Preface
Bruno Schulz, "The Mythologizing of Reality," *Letters and Drawings of Bruno Schulz*, edited by Jerzy Ficowski; translated by Walter Arndt and Victoria Nelson; preface by Adam Zagajewski (N.Y.: Fromm International Publishing Corp., 1990), pp. 115 & 116.

INFERNO epigrams:
Marinetti, Filippo Tommaso. *Marinetti: Selected Writings,* edited with an introduction by R.W. Flint; translated by R.W. Flint and Arthur A. Coppotelli (N.Y.: Farrar, Straus & Giroux, 1971), p. 44 & p. 107.

Canto 1 (36)
1. Coda [**It**, lit., tail, fr. **L** cauda] (ca. 1735) **1 a**: a concluding musical section that is formally distinct from the main structure **b**: a concluding part of literary or dramatic work **2**: something that serves to round out, conclude or summarize and that has an interest of its own. *Webster's Ninth New Collegiate Dictionary.* (Springfield, MA: Merriam Webster, Inc, 1991).

(1) (fig.) "Se il diavolo ci mette la coda, il diavolo ci ha messo la coda." = "Se, quando le cose vanno male, si complicano, non danno l'esito sperato." (2)(fig.) "Sapere dove il diavolo ha messo la coda." "Essere accorto." = "to be on the look-out", "to be careful." *Lo Zingarelli 1995* Vocabolario della lingua Italiana di Nicola Zingarelli, Dodicesima Edizione (Milano: Zingarelli, 1995).

CODA note: Plato, "Phaedrus," *Symposium and Phaedrus*, translated by Benjamin Jowett. (N.Y.: Dover Publications, Inc., 1993), p. 87.

Canto 2
Dante Alighieri, born in Florence, Italy, in 1265 died in exile in Ravenna in 1321. He is the author of *La Divina Commedia* (*Inferno, Purgatorio, and Paradiso*) and of course, the inspiration for this very humble new *Comedy*. Dante also wrote *La Vita Nuova* (The New Life), the *Convivio* (The Banquet), and *Monarchia* (Monarchy). See Allen Mandelbaum's masterful verse translation of *The Divine Comedy*, published by Bantam Books. This is the translation to get of the complete work; though I also recommend Daniel Halpern's *Dante's Inferno*, with translations by twenty major contemporary poets, and published by The Ecco Press.

Virgil—(or Vergilius Maro) was born in 70 BC near Mantua, and died in 19 BC. He is the author of *The Aeneid, The Eclogues*, and *The Georgics*. *The Aeneid*, Virgil's story of the founding of Rome, was a great source of inspiration for Dante. In fact, Book VI of Virgil's *Aeneid* anticipates the basic structure of Dante's *Commedia*. Virgil, of course, as everyone knows was Dante's (or the Master's) guide throughout the journey in the *Inferno*. See Allen Mandelbaum's National Book Award verse translation of *The Aeneid of Virgil* (1973), published by Bantam Books.

Captain N—A courageous rope walker as well as a master seaman and captain of a precarious bark in the perilous, godless seas of this world. He is also known as Nietzsche. He is this author's guide through much of <u>this</u> Inferno.

Nitel & Bim—Two relatively minor, but nonetheless powerful demons in the Inferno. If they had lived in the age of Virgil, they would have been inside the great Trojan horse that brought ruin and defeat to the citizens of Troy. Today they occupy a similar position. People don't see it because our 'horse,' though much larger, is invisible. For more on the story of the Trojan horse, see Book II of *The Aeneid of Virgil*.

CODA note: Gustave Flaubert, *The Temptation of St Antony*, translated w/introduction and notes by Kitty Mrosovsky (London/N.Y.: Penguin Books, 1983), p. 163.

Canto 3
SUMERCONS—These creatures make up to 85% of the population in the Inferno. They are terribly greedy, voracious, and materialistic. They are desiring-machines, in a constant quest of consumption. In fact, desire defines them. One should add, on their behalf, that one of the positive qualities of the SUMERCONS, is their politeness, as they always respond with a "thank you," whenever anyone praises something they own. This is because they completely identify themselves with the objects they possess. In other words, for them 'having' is equivalent to 'being'; objecthood and personhood being mere categories of the same ontology.

TISTARS—If the SUMERCONS identify themselves with the objects they possess, then the TISTARS define themselves by the objects—and spirit—they create. And while they may, to some extent, be ego invested—the possibility of at least escaping the prison house of the ego, remains a goal for a good number of them: their values being primarily spiritual rather than materialistic.

YAHOO(s)—At times the names YAHOOS and SUMER-CONS are used interchangeably here, and for the most part they are. However, it should be stressed, that the YAHOOS are much more voracious, greedy, and materialistic than the SUMERCONS. This voraciousness and avarice of the YAHOOS is such that at times it is difficult to differentiate these creatures–or demons–from the worst of the beasts. For more on the YAHOOS see Jonathan Swift, "A Voyage to the Country of the Houyhnhnms," *Gulliver's Travels*.

Canto 4
Arachne was a skillful weaver, who denied that the goddess Pallas was her teacher, and took offence to having art called 'divine.' In envy, anger, and revenge Pallas turned Arachne into a spider. See Ovid, "Book VI," *The Metamorphoses*, translated w/introduction by Horace Gregory (N.Y.: New American Library, 1958), pp. 163-167.

Phaethon—This is one of the most important gods in this Inferno, on equal par with Plutus. He is the immature god of a young nation, who lacking sufficient experience, and a historical sense of the world, threatens to destroy humanity. See Book II of Ovid's *Metamorphoses*, for the story of Phaethon's ride and fate.

CODA note: DEINOS is one of the gods of electricity. In this Inferno he is Phaethon's son.

Canto 5

Canto 6
Sisyphus—There are a number of versions of Sisyphus' punishment in Hades. What they all seem to agree on, is that Sisyphus was punished to ceaselessly roll the rock up the hill, only to have it roll down the hill again for all eternity, as a form of punishment for either attempting to steal the secrets of the gods, or for wanting to put Death in chains. "The workman of today works every day in his life at the same tasks, and this fate is no less absurd. But it is tragic only at the rare moments when it becomes conscious. Sisyphus, proletarian of the gods, powerless and rebellious, knows the whole extent of his wretched condition..." Albert Camus, "The Myth of Sisyphus," *The Myth of Sisyphus and Other Essays*, translated by Justin O'Brien (N.Y.: Vintage Books, 1955), p. 90.

Canto 7
King Wilhelm of the Gates—A very powerful and wealthy king who controls the micro world of electricity, atoms, simulacra, monetary exchange, and communication. He is one of the master builders of the invisible "Trojan horse." Yet, most importantly, King Wilhelm also controls the desires of SUMERCONS and YAHOOS.

Canto 8

Canto 8 1/2
Thamus–For more on the Egyptian god, Thamus, see the CODA in Canto 1.

Dulcinea is the beautiful and gentle woman—the goddess Don Quijote sees, when he looks at the smelly, toothless country woman. Miguel de Cervantes, *Don Quijote*.

Ojo!: Ojo is the Spanish word for eye (*occhio* in Italian), is also used as an expression to mean "observe, look, or watch!"

un altro film senza speranza—another film without hope.

CODA note: Dante, *La Vita Nuova*, translated w/introduction by Barbara Reynolds (London/N.Y.: Penguin Classics, 1969), p. 29. The number **9** is the number that Dante assigns to Beatrice. It is an important number for many reasons—the two most important for our purposes being, firstly that **9** is often seen as the number representing harmony or completeness in world cosmologies (e.g., the *ouroboros*—the serpent biting its tail is represented in Tibetan, Persian, Egyptian, and Arminian iconography as a number **9**); and secondly that it refers in Greek mythology, among many other things, to Zeus' creation of the **9** Muses. Ovid names only two in *The Metamorphoses*, Urania and Calliope; and Dante in similar fashion does the same in *La Vita Nuova*: mentioning Beatrice and *una donna gentile* who—like art and philosophy perhaps—distracts him from his contemplation of Beatrice. This is not to mention the obvious fact that the normal term for pregnancy is **9** months. What is clear is that the existence or non-existence of a real Beatrice is totally irrelevant—as Beatrice's importance for Dante is that of a neo-Platonic Form or Idea.

Canto 9
Edwin Abott, *Flatland: A Romance of Many Dimensions* (N.J.: Barnes & Noble, 1963).

RESMANIAC—The word RESMANIAC has its roots in the Latin *res* meaning *thing* and the Late Latin *maniacus*, from the

Greek *maniakos* meaning *mad(man)* (insane), this term refers to both a personality trait of SUMERCONS and YAHOOS, and to the very culture that produces the kind of creatures who madly go about acquiring material possessions. The frenetic wanting of things, stems from a deep, ingrained belief that things have *anima*—or souls, and that in possessing things the souls of things are transferred to the souls of the humans who own them. In short, YAHOOS and SUMERCONS make a fetish of every object they possess.

CODA note: Jonathan Swift, "A Voyage to the Country of the Houyhnhnms," *Gulliver's Travels, A Tale of a Tub, The Battle of the Books* (N.Y.: Modern Library, 1931), p. 297.

Canto 10
Scientia—Dante often distinguished between what he calls *scienz(i)a* and *sapienza*—that is to say, between knowledge and wisdom. This scholastic distinction probably originates in Augustine, who refers to *scientia*, as knowledge of temporal things, and *sapientia* as understanding of the eternal and the divine. "...There is a difference between the contemplation of eternal things and the action by which we use temporal things well: the former is called wisdom, the latter science." Saint Augustine, Book 12: Chapter 14, *The Trinity* (Washington, D.C.: The Catholic University of America Press, 1963), p. 363. Almost all religions make this distinction—a distinction that no one who lives in this Inferno of information cares anything about.

Canto 11
UTILSS OF LISTEAR—Most SUMERCONS and YAHOOS living in the Inferno also have membership in the culture of the UTILSS OF LISTEAR. In fact, one of the necessary attributes of a SUMERCON or YAHOO, is to possess the practical qualities of the UTILSS OF LISTEAR. Whatever cannot be nailed down, profited from, quantified, exchanged, manipulated, controlled, bent, or utilized for some material purpose or other, is not worthy of consideration. Marinetti is their god.

Correre a la morte—A line from *Purgatorio*, Canto XXXIII: 52-54. Dante is referring to those who live a life that is nothing more than a race to death.

CODA note: Marinetti, *Marinetti: Selected Writings* (N.Y.: Farrar, Straus & Giroux, 1971), p. 87.

Canto 12
CODA note: George Berkeley, Part I: #3, *A Treatise Concerning the Principles of Human Knowledge*. There are so many publications of this title, that it is meaningless to single out any one of them. Bishop George Berkeley (1685-1753), known for his idealist epistemology, was born and educated in Ireland; taught at Trinity College; lived for three years in Newport, Rhode Island, and was one of the early benefactors of Yale university. Besides his distinguished place in the history of philosophy, Berkeley also had a major influence on the American education system. The town of Berkeley in California is named after him.

Canto 13
Plutus is the Greek god of wealth. For the richest version of the myth of Plutus read Aritsophanes' *Plutus*. *The Complete Plays of Aristophanes*, edited w/introduction by Moses Hadas, *Plutus* translated by B.B. Rogers (N.Y.: Bantam Books, 1962), pp. 463-501.

Y2K—These two letters with the number 2 in the center were supposed to designate a world catastrophe caused by the short circuiting of our 'intelligent' electric machines, at the end of our second Christian millennium. No such thing happened, of course, since the coming catastrophe was invented by King Wilhelm of the Gates, Nitel & Bim, and all the others who supplied the electricity and owned the machines.

CODA note: Jean Chevalier & Alain Gheerbrant, *Dictionary of Symbols*, translated by John Buchanan-Brown (London: Penguin Books, 1996), pp. 764-765.

Canto 14
Chronos—This Chronos is a hybrid of Hesiod's Cronos (later the Roman Saturn) and Chronos (Father Time). Though the hybridization of these two figures did not take place until much later in Greek culture, the two are not completely unrelated. According to Hesiod's *Theogony*, Cronos, following his mother's wishes, castrated his father the Sky god, Ouranus (Heaven), and thereafter proceeded to eat all his children, to avoid escaping the same fate himself. But Rhea, who was both his sister and wife, fled to the island of Crete to give birth to their son (Zeus) who in time killed his own father (Cronos). This being the case then, Cronos' murder of his father, Ouranus, also marks the death of Heaven or Eternity: usher-

ing the temporal reality of human affairs. And thus out of Cronos' murder of Ouranus, Chronos (or Time) was born. Today Father Time eats his children—us—in the Inferno.

Technopoly is Neil Postman's term referring to RESMANIAC's control of human life—material, spiritual, and intellectual—through technology. Neil Postman, *Technopoly: The Surrender of Culture to Technology* (N.Y.: Vintage Books, 1993).

Lethe is the River of Forgetfulness in Hades. And the most important river in the culture of RESMANIAC. In Ovid's *Metamorphoses* Lethe flowed out of the Cave of Sleep, inducing drowsiness with its murmuring; and in the Master's *Commedia*, drinking water from Lethe freed the souls from the memory of their past sins. Since RESMANIAC has little or no history, and the memory of our past has become almost non-existent, drinking from Lethe makes it possible for our inhabitants to commit the most atrocious crimes with a perfectly good conscience. In fact, this lack of history—this lack of memory of everything that has gone before, contributes to RESMANIAC's lack of spiritual and human depth—as everyone here lives as though the present moment came from nowhere, without genesis. It was at least partly in answer to this condition that, the *Comedy* you are now reading, was written.

<u>Canto 15</u>
The Harrow is a machine of torture in Franz Kafka's short story, *In The Penal Colony*.

Locus Solus—Latin for Solitary Place.

CODA note: G.W.F. Hegel, *Phenomenology of Spirit*, translated by A.V. Miller, analysis and foreword J.N. Findlay (Oxford: Oxford University Press, 1977), pp. 61-62.

Canto 16
CODA note: Lao-tzu, *Tao Te Ching*, translated w/foreword & notes by Stephen Mitchell (N.Y.: Harper-Collins Publishers, 1988), p. 11.

Canto 17
POST-inferno—This term refers to the lack of gravity, weight, and meaning in our electric Inferno. It is an unfortunate result of the death of the One God, and the new religion of the text and simulation. In short, it is nothing else but one more form of nihilism.

For more on the Sicilian bull see the Master's *Inferno*, Canto XXVII:7-15.

Shoabusiness—"Many Israelis feel offended by the way in which the Holocaust is exploited in the Diaspora. They even feel ashamed that the Holocaust has become a civil religion for Jews in the United States...[of certain] writers, editors, historian, bureaucrats, and academics they say, using the word Shoa, which is Hebrew for Holocaust: 'There is no business like Shoa business.'" Jacobo Timerman, *The Longest War: Israel in Lebanon*, translated by Miguel Acoca (N.Y.: Alfred A. Knopf, 1982), p. 15.

Canto 18
The men in black, the well-dressed men, and the men in white refer to the following three periods of our millennium: 1425-1799, 1800-1874, 1875-present.

anthrapists are academicians who in the cold spirit of science record and retell the lives of Others, without taking the time to live and understand the subject of their study.

Prospero—The main character of Shakespeare's play, *The Tempest*, is the rightful Duke of Milan who controls everything and everyone in the island through magic—including the deformed, native slave, and personal servant, Caliban

Henri Pirenne, *Economic and Social History of Medieval Europe*, translated by I.E. Clegg (N.Y.: Harcourt, Brace & World, 1937), p. 21.

Canto 19
Ceres—daughter of Cronos and Rhea and grain goddess, she is one of the primordial goddesses who was there at the beginning. She is as Ovid called her in Book of V of *Metamorphoses*, "goddess of life-giving earth." She is one of the goddesses we are attempting to kill today through our own artificial metamorphoses.

Narcissus—As one of our gods, he is everywhere in RESMANIAC. Not being able to take his eyes away from his own reflection, he lives to look at himself in total self-absorption, incapable of love, dead to the world outside his ego. Phaethon and Narcissus are related in that both of them are young, selfish gods: one reckless and dangerous, the other passively lacking care and concern for the world.

Gaia is the broad breasted Earth, who with Ouranus gave birth to all of us. According to Hesiod, it was Gaia who had Cronus castrate his father, Ouranus. And since then, not out of revenge, but rather out of pride and stupidity, we have been doing whatever we can to destroy Gaia. She is one of the casualties of the Age of Electricity, the age of the white plague.

Minotaur—This monster with a man's body and a bull's head (the subject of many Picasso drawings), was the product of Pasiphae's mating with a white bull with a black spot between his horns. To hide the horror of this birth, King Minos got Daedalus to build the Labyrinth in which to imprison the Minotaur. And from then on, every nine years the Minotaur was fed 7 youths and maidens. Then one year, with the help of Ariadne's thread and torch, Theseus was able to enter the Labyrinth, slay the Minotaur, and find his way back out of the Labyrinth.

CODA note: J.P. Harpignies, *Double Helix Hubris: Against Designer Genes* (N.Y.: Cool Grove Press, 1997), pp. 8-9.

Canto 20
Metropolis N—What some refer to as the 'exciting' energy of Metropolis N is the result of an inexhaustible source of greed—a form of greed which the world has never before known: unique in all its evil. There is absolutely nothing that one may, even accidentally—in an unguarded moment of 'weakness'—call 'human' in this cold, electric city.

Babylon—Separated merely by time, and not much else, Metropolis N and Babylon are mirror images of each other: both, shameless whores. For a description of Babylon, which one can easily superimpose on the present reality of Metropolis N see John the Evangelist's *Book of Revelation*, Chapters 16: 19-20, 17, and 18. Especially significant is the section on "The Fall of Babylon." For a much clearer translation than the King James version see *The New American Bible* published by Collins World; translated by Members of the Catholic Biblical Association of America with informative footnotes. And for more on *The Book of Revelation*: J. Massyngberde Ford, *Revelation*, The Anchor Bible, Volume 38 (N.Y.: Doubleday, 1975).

Forasteros—Spanish word for strangers, or outsiders.

olvidados—Spanish for forgotten ones.

bodegas—Spanish for grocery store, or delicatessen. There are countless places like this all over Metropolis N...owned as well as frequented by people who in their search for a promised land, got lost in the dark woods, and ended up in the intestines of the city: without past, not truly living, and without future. So many lost 'Jesuses'.

CODA note: Henry Miller, "Megalopolitan Maniac," *Black Spring* (N.Y.: Grove Press, 1963), p. 203.

<u>Canto 21</u>
Cortona is a beautiful town in the south of Tuscany, sharing a border with the region of Umbria. It is the birthplace to artists

Luca Signorelli (1445-1523) and Gino Severini (1883-1966). The museum of the archdiocese of Cortona boasts of having in its permanent collection Fra Angelico's *Annuciazione*. The population of Cortona is about 22,000; its historical center about 2,000. For more information on this beautiful and friendly town, a good source is Frances Mayes' *Under the Tuscan Sun*.

Ravenna is in the eastern part of Emilia Romagna, bordering on Tuscany. It has a population of 136,000 people. And it is the city that Dante lived in during his years of exile, and where he died in 1321.

Belacqua—According to Allen Mandelbaum not much is known about Dante's friend, Belacqua, except for perhaps that he was a character witness by profession. Dante encounters Belacqua in Ante-Purgatory, as a late repentant who is too lazy to do what he must do—in other words, pray—to move from Ante-Purgatory to the next level of Purgatory. Samuel Beckett, an admirer of Dante, adopted Belacqua as the antihero of his short story "Sedendo et Quiescendo" and even more significantly of his early novel, *More Pricks Than Kicks*. To a great extent, one does not have to stretch the connection too far to find Belacqua even in Beckett's *Waiting for Godot*. For the section on Belacqua in *Purgatorio* see Canto IV: 115-135.

CODA note: Lewis Mumford, *The City in History: Its Origin, Its Transformation, and its Prospects* (N.Y.: Harcourt, Brace & World, 1961), p. 312.

Canto 22
POST-Inferno–See note for Canto 17.

Canto 23
Geryon—This multi-headed monster is killed by Hercules; he is described in *The Book of Revelation* in a variety of ways, and is encountered by Dante in Canto 17: 1-15 of the *Inferno*. Dante who associates Geryon with fraud, describes it as having the face of a man, the body of a serpent, and a pointed tail (*coda*). See Canto 1 for the definition and other cultural associations of the word *coda*.

Thomas More—Born in England in 1477, author of *Utopia*, he was a humanist scholar and churchman, and a man of principles who was executed in 1535 by Henry VIII for refusing to accept the King as the supreme head of the Church of England. The film *A Man For All Seasons* is about the last years of his life.

Susanna (and the elders)—The story of Susanna and the Elders is the story of a married woman who is propositioned by the elders of her town. She refuses their advances, and is unjustly accused by the very same elders of adultery. It is only through the help of Daniel who cross-examines the elders separately that the truth is revealed, and Susanna is proven innocent, while the elders are found guilty of lying and deceit. The story of Susanna, one of the stories of the Apocrypha, can be found in the Greek version of the Bible, as Chapter 13 of *The Book of Daniel*. It is not to be found in the King James version.

Canto 24
Apollo, one of the most important gods in the pantheon, is the god of light and artistic inspiration. He is also identified with Helios, or the Sun: thereby often referred to as a Sun god. The name Apollo is used interchangeably with the name Phoebus by certain writers like Ovid and Homer. Being the god of light, no other god seems to hold a higher place than Apollo for Dante. In fact, it is not the Judeo-Christian god whose name he invokes on first entering Paradiso, but rather Apollo (*Paradiso*, Canto 1: 13).

Beatrice—The beautiful, the eternal feminine, the earthly and the heavenly in one, the inspiration, the subject of *La Vita Nuova*, and the Master's guiding light through Paradiso is—despite all claims made by academicians—the Master's version of a Platonic Form or Idea: of Beauty, of Divine Wisdom, and Love. To equate Beatrice with a flesh and blood person who lived at such and such a time, in such and such a place, is a foolish and worthless undertaking. To understand who Beatrice was for Dante, read Plato's *Symposium* and *Phaedrus*; Plotinus' *The Enneads*; and Ficino's *Commentary on Plato's Symposium on Love*.

BRUNO refers to the Polish writer and artist, BRUNO SCHULZ (1892-1942). Known in the United States as the author of two short works of fiction, *The Street of Crocodiles* (N.Y.: Penguin Books, 1977), and *Sanatorium Under the Sign of the Hourglass* (N.Y.: Walker & Company, 1978), his work has been championed by such writers as Philip Roth and Cynthia Ozick. The latter whose novel *The Messiah of Stockholm* (N.Y.: Vintage Books, 1988) deals with Schulz' long lost manuscript of *The Messiah*—the book he was working on before he died. What is usually not acknowledged or mentioned about Schulz is that he was also a wonderful artist who did a series of powerful drawings dealing with the subject of masochism and foot fetishism, published under the title, *The Booke of Idolatry*: creating his own myths as well as returning to classical Greek mythology for an exploration of the theme of power and submission. Bruno Schulz earned his living as a high school teacher of arts and crafts in his native town of Drohobycz, in the region of Poland known then as Galicia. In 1941 the Nazis marched into Drohobycz; and one Gestapo officer who took a liking to his drawings turned BRUNO into his "artist slave," providing him with food and protection in exchange for drawings. He lived this way for a little over a year, and then one day, on a day in November the Jews of Drohobycz would come to call "Black Thursday", Schulz retruning home with a loaf of bread under his arm, was shot in the head by an SS officer. He was buried by a friend in the Jewish cemetery. The location of his grave is unknown.

Circe—The two famous versions of the myth of Circe are found in Homer's Book X of *The Odyssey* and in Ovid's Book XIV of *The Metamorphoses*. Upon Odysseus' (Homer) or Ulysses' (Ovid) arrival in the island, Circe, the enchanting goddess welcomes Ulysses' men with a potion which turns them into pigs.

> *Then with a blue stole thrust across her shoulders,*
> *Ran through her palace where pigs, dogs, and lions*
> *Leaped up to kiss her feet as she swept by.*
> --From *The Metamorphoses*, p.384.

It was this aspect of animal-like submission and foot fetishism which made its way into the drawings of Bruno Schulz. For BRUNO'S own version of the myth of Circe see *The Divine Duty of Servants: A Book of Worship* (N.Y.: Cool Grove Press, 1999).

Eurylochus is one of the characters in the myth of Circe, who remains firm and runs back to Ulysses' ship for help.

Zeus—Born of Cronos and Rhea in the island of Crete, he is considered God of the gods, and the god of thunder and lightning. Just as Cronos killed his children, Zeus in turn killed Cronos, his father. Because Zeus is the god of thunder and lightning, he is for us one of the gods of electricity: vengeful, powerful, a sky god—his power always comes from above to either bring destruction or to end any sign of rebellion. He was present in Hiroshima and Nagasaki. And most recently he was the oppressive god who punished the rebels of Tianamen Square.

Cythera—This name comes from a town in Crete, or from the island of Cythera, where Aphrodite (born of the castrated sex organs of Ouranus) first appeared when she rose from the sea. "There she stepped out, a goddess, tender and beautiful, and round her slender feet the green grass shot up. She is called Aphrodite by gods and men, because she grew in the froth, and also Cytherea, because she was born in watery Cythera, and the Cyprian, because she was born in watery Cyprus." Hesiod, *Theogony*, translated w/introduction by Norman O. Brown (Indiana: Bobbs-Merrill Educational Publishing, 1953), p.58. This was another myth which Bruno Schulz explored in his artwork. In fact, one of his drawings is entitled *On Cythera*. And given Hesiod's description of Aphrodite's slender feet, it is hard to imagine Schulz's knowledge of the myth of Cythera not coming directly from this passage in the *Theogony*.

CODA note: Manilius, *Astronomica*, translated by G.P. Gold (Cambridge, MA: Harvard University Press, 1977), Book 2: 903-928, p. 155 & Book 4: 574-598, p. 269.

Canto 25
Iesu—The Greek name for Jesus.

Dike–The Greek word for justice.

BAKU—This large island lies 77 miles southwest of Prospero's island: sharing a similar early history with the latter, while having a much less fortunate fate. Its Tyrant, whose ancestry has its origin in Prospero's magnificent continent, rules over his people by castrating the human spirit through fear and terror.

Horai—These are the Hours or Seasons in Hesiod. They are spirits of limits, and as such they represent just government and peace.

CODA note: Chevalier & Gheerbrant, *Dictionary of Symbols*, Brown: p. 795 & Red: p. 127.

Canto 26
Dante, *Monarchia/Monarchy*, translated by Prue Shaw (Cambridge: Cambridge University Press, 1996). See Book II, Section iii for Dante's justification of Roman world domination through divine right.

Samuel/Sam refers to Samuel Beckett who was highly influenced by Dante's work; and especially by the *Commedia*.

Mr. Bloom—or simply Bloom, is the protagonist of James Joyce's epic novel, *Ulysses*.

CODA note: Deidre Bair, *Samuel Beckett: A Biography* (N.Y.: Harcourt Brace Jovanovich, 1978), p. 308.

Canto 27
>*Hamm: Nature has forgotten us.*
>*Clov: There's no more nature.*

The above lines of dialogue come from Samuel Beckett, *Endgame* (N.Y.: Grove Weidenfeld, 1958), p. 11.

Logos—The Greek word for Reason.

Metatron (one who occupies the throne next to the divine one)—In *Genesis* 5:22, Metatron who is often equated with Enoch (of the apocryphal *Book of Enoch*), was transformed from human to angel when he ascended to heaven: where he served as God's scribe recording the deeds of men. According to the *Encyclopedia Judaica* (Volume 11, p. 1444), in the *Talmud's* version, Metatron was given permission to sit beside God because he was the heavenly scribe who recorded the "good deeds of Israel."

Occhi—The Italian word for 'eyes'.

Roland—(etymologically, famous land) is the heroic knight of the 11th century French poem *Chanson de Roland* (*Song of*

Roland), who defeated the Saracens at Roncesvalles. He is one of the heroes of the Charlemagne cycle of legends, as well as the subject of Ariosto's epic poem, *Orlando Furioso*.

Beowulf is the hero of the British medieval legend *Beowulf* who slays the monster, Grendel: nocturnal devourer of King Hrothgar's men. Beowulf kills both Grendel and his mother in a great triumphant struggle fought at the bottom of the lake. The poem was recorded by an unknown monk in the eighth century. See *Beowulf*, translated by Seamus Heaney (N.Y.: Farrar, Straus & Giroux, 2000).

Grendel—For the 'monster's' point of view see John Gardner's magnificent novel and retelling of the legend, *Grendel*, reissued by Vintage Books.

CODA note: For an excellent English rendition of Arthur Rimbaud's *Une Saison En Enfer* read Louise Varese's translation of *A Season in Hell* and *The Drunken Boat*, published in a bilingual edition by New Directions. The original of this quote and Varese's translation can be found on opposing pages 76 and 77.

Canto 28
Prometheus is the rebellious Titan, who stole the Fire from the gods and gave it to humans. Zeus punished Prometheus by having a vulture eat away at his liver every day. Every night his liver was restored, only to be eaten by the vulture again the following day. His punishment resembles the punishment of Sisyphus.

Pandora, or the first woman (created by Zeus), is Greek mythology's version of Eve. Given a box and told not to open it, she disobeyed and opened it, allowing all the evils of the world to escape. Hope was all that remained in the box when she closed it again. Pandora was the wife of Epimetheus, Prometheus' brother.

Faust—This character comes from an actual historical figure by the name of Dr. Johann Faustus, a German physician accused of being a magician, and an accomplice of the devil. In many ways, Faust is Pandora's twin brother, whose desire to know is greater than his faith in God. For it is his unquenchable thirst for knowledge (*scientia*) which leads him to sign a contract with Lucifer—through Mephistopheles—Lucifer's cunning intermediary on earth. The two most famous versions of the myth of Faust are Marlowe's play *Dr. Faustus* and Goethe's epic poem, *Faust*.

Alcibiades is one of the participants in Plato's *Symposium*; a lover of Socrates.

Comte de Lautreamont, *Les Chants de Maldoror*, translated by Guy Wernham (N.Y.: New Directions Publishing Corp., 1946).

Marsyas is the artist; the flute player who challenged Apollo (Latona's son) to a contest, wherein he played the flute and Apollo played his lyre. Marsyas lost the contest, and Apollo had him tied to a tree and flayed alive until he died. The most moving and horrifying account of Marsyas' cruel fate can be found in Book VI of Ovid's *Metamorphoses*. Marsyas cries out: "Why do you strip myself from me/O I give in, I lose, forgive me now..." (p. 174).

CODA note: *The Song of God: Bhagavad-Gita*, translated by Swami Prabhavananda and Christopher Isherwood; Introduction by Aldous Huxley (N.Y.: New American Library, 1944), pp. 21-22.

<u>Canto 29</u>
Bartleby is the main character of Herman Melville's short story, *Bartleby the Scrivener*. One day Bartleby decides that he no longer cares to perform the office duties typically demanded of him, and from that day on whenever his supervisor asks him to perform a certain task Bartleby responds by saying "I would prefer not to."

Johnny (or John) Sims is the 'average' hero of King Vidor's brilliant 1928 film, *The Crowd*. Johnny Sims' enthusiasm for New York City life, begins with a trip to Coney Island, but is soon after crushed by the tragic death of his daughter, all kinds of family pressures, and the humiliation of unemployment. By the end of the film, the vanquished Sims is reduced to playing the ukelele for money in the midst of the crowd. This early film captures in an impressionistic and heart rending way the great American myth of success gone wrong. James Murray, the actor who played Sims died a few years later, much like the character he played, in dire poverty. He fell and drowned in the Hudson River, as no one jumped in to rescue him, thinking that he was play-acting.

SPERA—In the Italian of Petrarca, this word meant "to wait," or "to hope." Here SPERA is the goddess of the Purgatorio.

CODA note: Jerry Mander, *Four Arguments For The Elimination of Television* (N.Y.: Quill, 1978), p. 200.

Canto 30
Zeno of Elea (450 B.C.)—This Greek pre-Socratic philosopher is known for his paradoxes concerning plurality and movement. Though only fragments of his book are left to us through Aristotle's *Physics*, one of the most interesting examples of his paradoxes—or dichotomy—deals with the logical impossibility of motion. According to Zeno, motion was impossible because in order for an object to cover any distance it would first have to cover half the distance, then half that...and half that...and half that...and so on to infinity....So that an arrow projected from a bow would actually never reach its destination, or to put it more dramatically, would never leave position A—or its place in the bow.

Jacob's ladder—"When he [Jacob] came upon a certain shrine, as the sun had already set, he stopped there for the night. Taking one of the stones at the shrine, he put it under his head and lay down to sleep at that spot. Then he had a dream: a stairway [or ladder] rested on the ground, with its top reaching to the heavens; and God's messengers were going up and down on it." *Genesis* 28:11-12.

Sedendo et quiescendo—This is the title of one of Beckett's Belacqua short stories. It has its origin in a sentence from Thomas à Kempis' *Imitation of Christ*. The original Latin sentence reads: *Sedendo et quiescendo anima efficitur prudens*—or what is nearly the English equivalent: "In sitting and in silence the soul acquires wisdom."

CODA note: The dialogue cited here is from the published translation of the film script of *Alphaville*. Jean-Luc Godard,

Alphaville, translated by Peter Whitehead (N.Y.: Simon & Schuster, 1966), pp. 38-39.

PARADISO epigrams:
Leonard Cohen, "The Future", *The Future*; Columbia Records. Lyrics written and copyrighted by Leonard Cohen, Stranger Music, Inc.(BMI).

Brazilian folk song quoted from P.M., *Bolo'Bolo* (N.Y.: Semiotext(e), 1985), p. 1.

Canto 31
Buddha means the enlightened or the awakened one. This was the title given to Siddhartha Gautama, a religious leader much like Christ—conceived both as mythical as well as a historical figure. He is said to have lived some time around 566-486 B.C. Like Simon of the desert, who in his ascetic isolation in the desert was tempted and tested by beautiful, enticing women, Siddhartha was similarly tested by Mara (desire) while lying under the Bodhi tree of wisdom. In Siddhartha's refusal to be tempted by Mara, he attained enlightenment, or buddhahood. While sitting under the Bodhi tree he came to understand the following four noble truths: 1) that existence is unhappiness, 2) that the unhappiness of the world is the product of desire, 3) that desire can be overcome, and 4) that the way to overcome desire is through the Eightfold Path. The last of which has to do with the correct balance between understanding (*sapienza*) and action.

Krishna—In Hindu mythology Krishna is the divine incarnation of Vishnu. Krishna is the Brahman in *The Song of God*, or

The Bhavavad-Gita. Like Virgil and then Beatrice in the *Commedia*, Krishna is a spiritual guide for Arjuna in the *Gita*. Like Christ, like Beatrice, like Siddhartha, etc., Krishna warns Arjuna about the traps of desire, while making a distinction between knowledge of the world and wisdom, but renouncing neither completely. As Krishna rightly teaches Arjuna: *Action rightly renounced brings freedom/Action rightly performed brings freedom.* (p. 57)

DIRTEC—The monetary currency of the Purgatorio.

Der wille zur macht—German for "the will to power." *The Will to Power* is also the title of one of Nietzsche's books.

CODA note: "The Yoga of Knowledge," *Bhagavad-Gita*, pp. 43-44.

Canto 32
Tantalus—Invited to a banquet by the gods, the cruel Tantalus killed his son and served him for dinner, in order to prove that the gods could not tell the difference between human and animal flesh. But the gods did know, and did not fall for it; except for Demeter who unbeknownst to her, consumed part of the boy's shoulder. The gods punished Tantalus for questioning their knowledge and wisdom, by banishing him to the lower regions of hell, where in Dante-like fashion, he was placed in water up to his neck and whenever he tried to drink to quench his thirst, the water would recede away from him. And then whenever he tried to eat from a tree nearby the fruits would disappear. Hence the word tantalize. See Homer's version of this tale in *The Odyssey*, Book XI, translated by Robert Fagles; introduction and notes by Bernard Fox (N.Y.: Viking, 1996), lines 669-680, pp. 268-269.

tantalize—[Tantalus] vt. (1597): to tease or torment by or as if by presenting something desirable to the view but continually keeping it out of reach...
—*Webster's Ninth New Collegiate Dictionary*

The Tower of Babel—Threatened by the accomplishments of man in building a tower to reach the heavens, Yahweh decides to put an end to this human project by giving humanity a multiplicity of languages, which will make communication between human beings impossible. This is the *Old Testament* myth of the different languages spoken in the world. This is one of those justifications that Biblical monotheism has to resort to in order to make itself logically coherent. See *Genesis* 11:1-9.

"O buono Apollo"—*Paradiso*, Canto 1: 13.

CODA note: Giovanni Pico della Mirandola, *Oration on the Dignity of Man*, translated by A. Robert Caponigri (Chicago, IL: Regnery Gateway, 1956), pp. 18-19.

Canto 33
Penia—The Greek word for poverty. For an excellent treatment of *Penia* as the necessary balance of Plutus, see Aristophanes' play, *Plutus*: comic and insightful.

Midas—This is the ancient Greek version of the Genie in the bottle myth. Dionysus granting Midas anything he wished, Midas responded by asking that whatever he touched be turned to gold. And so it happened that whatever Midas touched immediately turned to gold. The problem with this,

Midas soon discovered, was that even his food turned to gold. Midas is certainly a RESMANIAC god. And some day, like Midas, the YAHOOS and SUMERCONS of RESMANIAC will have to wash in their own unpolluted river—if such a river indeed exists—to renounce the initial wish. The RESMANIAC expression "the Midas touch" has its origin in this myth.

CODA note: E.M. Forster, "The Machine Stops," *The Science Fiction Hall of Fame, Volume IIB*, edited by Ben Bova (N.Y.: Avon Books, 1973), p. 276 & p. 278.

Canto 34
Arcadia—An ideal, pastoral city in Greek mythology. It is Virgil's ideal city in *The Eclogues*. See Guy Lee's translation of Virgil's *The Eclogues* (Penguin Books, 1980); and for more on Virgil's Arcadia an excellent source is M. Owen Lee, *Death and Rebirth in Virgil's Arcadia* (N.Y.: SUNY Press, 1989).

Marsilio refers to Marsilio Ficino (1433-1499), Italian Neo-Platonist philosopher, author of the famous treatise on Love in Plato's Symposium. He was the son of Cosimo de Medici's personal physician, and he was employed by the Medici family to translate the works of Plato from Greek into Latin. His work on love inspired a number of Neo-Platonist philosophers, like the Portuguese Neo-Platonist writer, Leon Hebreo. For an English translation of Ficino's *De Amore*: Marisilio Ficino, *Commentary on Plato's Symposium on Love*, translated w/introduction and notes by Sears Jayne (Connecticut: Spring Publications,1985).

Diotima instructs Socrates on the different kinds and levels of love in *The Symposium*.

Dionysus is the famous Greek god of fertility, sex, and wine. Dionysian rites were often orgiastic in nature, leading at times to either animal or human sacrifices. Nietzche opposes the Dionysian and Apollonian spirit to each other in The *Birth of Tragedy*, interpreting the latter as the rational, orderly aspect of humanity and the former—the Dionysian, the Dithyrambic—as the emotional and the irrational, and by that token, the more primordial and important aspect of the two. In fact, for Nietzsche, reason is merely an offshoot of the irrational and desire.

CODA note: J.G. Ballard, *The Unlimited Dream Company* (London: Jonathan Cape, 1979), p. 176. This beautiful novel by Ballard remains in obscurity, and unfortunately, out of print.

INFERNO Revisited epigram:
Fyodor Dostoevsky, "The Dream of A Ridiculous Man," *The Best Short Stories of Dostoevsky*, translated by David Magarshack (N.Y.: The Modern Library, 1992), p. 342, p. 343 & p. 348.

<u>Canto 35</u>
The line "give me back the Berlin wall…" is a line from the song by Leonard Cohen entitled "The Future."

Cogito ergo inferno—"I think therefore inferno."

CODA note: T.S. Elliot, "Little Gidding," *Four Quartets* (N.Y.: Harcourt, Brace & World, Inc., 1943), p.58.

List of Illustrations

1. *Il fondo dell'inferno* by Michele Perillo, p. 2.
2. *Filippo Argenti* by Michele Perillo, p. 6
3. Porno on TV by Rolando Perez p. 21
4. Detail of Masonic symbol from American dollar bill, p. 31.
5. *Immersione nel Lete* by Michele Perillo, p. 37.
6. Dead Soldier image on TV by Rolando Perez, p. 44.
7. Engravings from *Compendium Maleficarum* by Francesco Maria Guazzo, p. 63.
8. Zodiac man, Fifteenth century German woodcut, p. 67.
9. Detail from *Belacqua* by Michele Perillo, p. 92.
10. *I cerchi mobili* by Michele Perillo, p. 102.
11. *Visione di Beatrice* by Michele Perillo, p. 108.
12. Ouroboros (source unknown), p. 116.

Back cover:

I simoniaci by Michele Perillo

About The Author

Cuban born, Rolando Perez, is the author of numerous books on a variety of subjects ranging from philosophy and literary criticism to poetry and drama. Some of his published titles include *The Divine Duty of Servants* published by Cool Grove Press, *On An(Archy) and Schizoanalysis, Severo Sarduy and the Religion of the Text, The Odyssey,* and *The Lining of Our Souls* (based on selected paintings of Edward Hopper.) He has also written over 15 plays that have received production in NYC.

Mr. Perez has a B.A. in philosophy from Trenton State College, an M.A. in philosophy, an M.A. in Spanish (both from Stony Brook), and a Masters in Library Science from Rutgers University. He is a librarian and the Philosophy and Romance Languages bibliographer at Hunter College.